TALLY AND THE

ANGEL

By

ELEANOR DIXON

BOOK ONE: INDIA

Copyright © 2021 by Eleanor Dixon
Published by Burreau Publishing 2021

Gorsky Road, Shropshire TF9 2JD

Print Book ISBN: 978-1-8382708-1-0

Front Cover design and illustration: Rob Bennet

This is a work of fiction. Names, characters, places and incidents are either the products of the author's imagination or used in a fictitious manner. Any resemblance to actual persons, living or dead is purely coincidental.

For Hazel,
who is just a kiss away

PROLOGUE

Tally raced into the airport departure hall, not caring that she was acting more like a six-year-old than a nearly-thirteen-year-old. The excitement was unbearable! This would be her first trip on a plane.

No good waiting for Dad; he was walking far too slowly. She ran to the centre of the vast hall, dodging people, trolleys and suitcases, and skidded to a halt, oblivious of the hurrying passengers who tutted and swerved around her.

It was amazing! There was so much noise, so many colours, so many people. She twirled round, glowing as she gazed at them all. Some were dressed in winter woollies and must be heading for the snow; some were dressed in lighter, brighter clothes, surely destined, like her, for warmer climes. There were businessmen hurrying along in suits, mums with babies in pushchairs, people of all nationalities scrutinising the electronic boards or kissing loved ones goodbye. There was so much to look at. She wanted to hug herself; it was so exhilarating.

But then that familiar wave of sadness crept up to remind her why she'd never been on a plane before, and she felt slightly guilty at letting herself forget. Somewhat more soberly, she turned round to search for her dad, whom she'd left to battle with the trolley and suitcases. There he was. His expression was empty and his eyes slightly glassy. It just wasn't right - he looked so lonely without Mum. The last traces of Tally's excitement snuffed out like a candle. In her mind she was back in the chapel of rest, watching the curtain draw around her mum's coffin. She squeezed her eyes shut to wipe out the scene. What had Mum ordered her to do? 'Be happy, Tally, be happy'.

She took a deep breath. So that's what she would do.

Tally ran to her dad and slipped one hand into his, while reaching up to cradle the pendant at her throat with the other.

CHAPTER ONE

One week earlier.

"Few know me. I have remained hidden for thousands of years."

Tally jumped at the knock on her bedroom door and hastily wiped her eyes on the corner of the duvet.

"Come in," she croaked, forcing herself to sit up and sound as normal as possible, though she didn't think she'd made a great job of it.

Aaron Carter came in. "Already in bed, poppet?"

Tally nodded, and as she looked up into her dad's haggard face she wanted to cry all over again. He sat next to her and she burrowed under his arm to lay her cheek against his chest, deriving some comfort from the warmth rising through his jumper. He stretched his legs out along the top of the duvet, beside her own underneath.

In his hand was a small box and an envelope. Tally wanted to ask about them but didn't trust her voice not to crack.

Dad spoke first. "We'll be all right, kiddo," he whispered. "It's good to cry, but Mum would have preferred us to be happy. So after today, let's try to put on a brave face, shall we?"

Tally didn't want to put on a brave face. She just wanted to disappear under her duvet and cry till she fell asleep and then not feel anything. How could she be brave when she would never see her beautiful, gentle mother again? Didn't anyone understand how it felt? Even though her mum, once a ballerina, had been ill for months, and Tally had had time to get used to the idea that she would die, she had never really believed it, never allowed herself to picture how life would be once that terrible thing happened.

She drew a shuddery breath and nodded into Dad's chest. For a few minutes neither of them spoke; he just squeezed her tight. Eventually he said, "Tal, I have something for you," as he extricated himself from her fierce hug. He held up the box and envelope. "But first, let me tell you something I think might cheer you up."

He put the two items on the bedside table.

Tally sat up and wriggled round on the bed so she faced him. It didn't look as if what Dad wanted to say was going to be cheery - his face was grey; he looked as if he was in agony. Tally swallowed her apprehension. Her heart began to pound, and her breath shortened like she'd been running.

Dad scanned her face. "Deep breaths, sweetheart," he murmured, "Don't panic. It's nothing bad," he added dubiously. Then, so quietly that Tally almost didn't hear him, "Perhaps it's not the right moment. I never was very good at timing."

He sighed and spoke in a rush, like Tally did when she was afraid that if she didn't say everything all at once she'd lose her nerve.

"The thing is, your mum and I talked a lot about what I would do once she'd gone, and I've made some decisions. I've taken a sabbatical from the hospital and -"

"What's a sabbatical?" Tally interrupted, finding her voice at last.

"It's a period of paid leave," Dad explained. "They have allowed me a year under the circumstances – theoretically I should get two as I've been there for fourteen years, but times are hard..." He tilted his head to check she'd understood, and she nodded cautiously.

"Anyway..." Dad clenched his fists, as if what he was about to say was hurting him. "Mum and I could see how much you love school and I'd hate to drag you away from it, but I really want to travel. As you know, Mum travelled lots when she was dancing, but after we had you she didn't want to. And then we couldn't because of her illness. But it's always been my dream, and we talked about how it would be the best thing for me to do once she'd... gone." He took a big shuddery breath.

Tally held her breath. Where would they go?

Dad was continuing. "Of course, it would be the hardest thing on earth to leave you, but I understand how you wouldn't want to quit the school you love – all your friends, your activities, your schoolwork. Especially as you're doing so well, top of the class and all that." Tally felt the blood drain out of her face. "So Mum and I decided to let you be a boarder."

Tally gasped. Dad faltered. "Is that a smiley and a thumbs up?" he asked. Then he frowned. "I'm afraid it wouldn't be straight away. I couldn't bear to part from you just yet. But I was thinking maybe next term. Once things have calmed down a bit and we've got used to… to life being different."

Tally was sure her heart had found its way to the bottom of her stomach. But Dad was rushing on. "Of course, in the holidays you'd fly out to wherever I am. If you want to, that is. Or I would come back and we'd spend them here. We'd still see as much of each other – just not daily. I'd miss you like crazy, but I do understand that you'd rather be with friends of your own age and in a school you love."

Tally stared at him, speechless. School she loved? She absolutely hated it. And she had no friends; the other girls ignored her and called her a swot because she was always top of the class. They were always getting together at the weekends to go shopping or to the cinema and never invited her to join in. They huddled in groups in corridors, giggling about boys and make-up, then stopped talking when she walked by, only to screech with laughter after she'd gone past. Love it? She never wanted to see the place again, never mind stay there day and night for weeks on end. She had mentioned none of this during Mum's illness, of course. But secretly she had hoped, once it was all over, she'd be able to persuade Dad to let her go to a normal state school instead of the private academy.

Finding her voice at last, she croaked, "You can't. You can't leave me too. Please, Daddy, please don't leave me." She gripped the duvet, twisting the fabric.

Dad stared at her in horror. "I'm not talking about going right now, Tally. In a few months or so, I was thinking. And I wouldn't be *leaving* you – I'd just be away during term time. I thought you'd love it. It wouldn't be much different to now – I'm always so busy at the hospital and you're usually in bed by the time I get home."

"I couldn't stand it!" Tally cried. "Mum's gone, and you'd go too. I'd be all alone, like an orphan. And in that hateful school! Please don't make me go back! It's the worst place in the world. Please, please, please, Daddy, don't do it." The hot tears started to stream down her already red and sore cheeks, but she did nothing to stop them.

Her father scooped her into his arms and squeezed her tight. "What's all this?" he asked, amazed. "What hateful school?"

Between sniffles and gulps, Tally tried to explain to him how she had become an outcast among the other girls, and that spending her time studying and doing well in her lessons was the only thing left for her to do because no one talked to her during the break times.

Dad's distress made his voice raspy. "We had no idea! We thought you were so happy there. Have you been keeping all this secret for Mum's sake?"

Tally nodded miserably.

"Oh, Tally!" Dad breathed. "How could you be so grown up? That was so brave!"

Tally shuddered. "I heard mum telling Auntie Jayne that she would feel so much better if she knew I was happy," she whispered. "So I pretended. To make her better. But it didn't work. She didn't get better," she finished miserably.

Dad stared at the duvet, his eyes slightly wet. "Well, this changes everything!" he said at last. "Of course I won't go, my darling. I'll go back to the hospital and we'll find a different school for you, don't you worry about that. We'll carry on as normal. I never imagined..." He swallowed.

Tally felt a stab of guilt. Dad must have spent ages perfecting his plan, thinking she would jump at it.

"Why can't we go travelling together?" she choked suddenly.

"But Tally, you have to go to school!" Dad exclaimed, lifting his dark eyes to gaze into her clear blue ones.

"Do I?" The glimmer of an idea had formed in Tally's mind and she grasped it. "Why? Why can't you teach me? Lots of people are home schooled. We'd travel, and you'd tutor me as we go along." Thoughts tumbled around her head as her brainwave took on a life of its own.

"It would be fantastic," she breathed. "We'd do lessons in the morning and sightseeing in the afternoons. I'd learn far more than in a classroom, and I'd work really, really hard. I would do everything you said and wouldn't let you down - I'd do all the homework you set me, never ask to watch TV, never complain about having to study anything, never be a nuisance, ne..."

"Whoa, whoa, whoa!" Dad put up his hands to stop her. He stood up and walked over to the window. Tally held her breath.

Dad turned round and looked at her, his eyes heavy with grief. "I don't know, sweetheart," he said. "This has all come as such a shock. I can't quite get my head round it. Leave it with me. But don't press me."

It was as much as Tally could hope for, and anyway, at least he hadn't totally trashed her idea. But then, he was like that, her dad. He always had time for her, and always gave his full attention to anything she said. Perhaps being a consultant surgeon made him more thoughtful and willing to listen to other people. Or maybe he had become such a good doctor because of his considerate nature. Whatever! Mentally Tally crossed her fingers. She would have to wait and see.

"Now," he said, picking up the two mysterious items he'd brought in with him, "this envelope and gift are from Mum. She insisted that I wait till after the funeral to give it to you, and she gave me strict instructions that you had to read the letter before you open the box."

Tally stretched out a shaking hand and took the two treasures from her dad. The box measured about the size of her fist and was made of a beautiful, orange wood. It glowed warmly, as though someone had polished it daily for generations. The cream envelope was thick and heavy in an old-fashioned way.

"I'll leave you to it," Dad murmured as he dropped a kiss on her forehead and stood up. "Don't worry about anything. We'll work it out. Call me if you need me – otherwise I'll see you in the morning."

"Night, Dad," said Tally, letting out a long-held breath. He closed the door and she turned over the envelope. Tears stung again as she read her name scrawled across it in her mum's rather untidy handwriting: Miss Natalie Carter.

CHAPTER TWO

"My name means Beauty of God, and He created me in the beginning – before water, light, sound. Before mountains and seas. He created all of us and gave us parts to play in this fresh world. He put Eleleth in charge of perfection and peace; Eassiel to preside over solitude and tears. There are so many of us – I cannot tell you all their names and all their roles."

"'Wherever you are,
I am just a kiss away'.

My darling Tally,

Please don't cry, my big brave girl. Although you can't see me anymore, I am still with you. I am in the air, the flowers, the very essence of everything around you. If you want to talk to me, just pick a daisy or look up into the trees – I will be there.

Do you remember when you were about six, and you used to love going to parties? You never wanted to leave. Yet when you got home to a mug of creamy hot chocolate, a snuggly bed, and a bedtime story, you forgot all about it and couldn't be happier.

Well, that's a bit what it's like for me. I didn't want to leave our party, but now I am cuddled up in my own cosy bed and my bedtime story is you, my darling – your life and what you do from here on will keep me enthralled as it unfolds, chapter by chapter. So make it a splendid one, my Tally; make me want to keep turning the pages. Enjoy every single moment, every single thing. Take care of Daddy, but live your life. Remember me, but don't be sad.

We had so much more than most ever have. Remember that and be happy.

Now for the box. In my youth, before I met your dad, I travelled a lot– yes, honestly! I know you find that strange as I have always been so content to stay put, potter in the garden and be with my lovely husband and daughter. But when I was dancing, I toured to some incredible places. It was during that time I learned to love my home and appreciate what I have, rather than search for something else. That doesn't mean you mustn't go out and search – you must! I had my lessons to learn; you have yours.

Inside the wooden case you will find Jophiel. A traveller gave him to me when I was in Egypt. Open it now, darling, and take him out before you read any more."

Tally desperately wanted to keep on reading her mum's words. It was almost like she was in the room with her, and she wanted to hold on to that feeling. But she obeyed, put the letter down and opened the box.

As the lid came off, she stared in awe. Lying on a bed of midnight blue velvet was a pendant of an angel which shone so brightly it was as if there was a light inside. It looked like it was made of some sort of white stone. Although it was only as big as her thumb, someone had carved each detail of his face and robes in minute detail. Every feather of the luxurious arched wings that rose behind his head and framed his body looked as if a sculptor had applied them individually. His hands rested gently by his sides, with palms facing loosely up in a gesture that said 'welcome'.

Dare she touch it? Mum had said 'take him out' but Tally was too awed to pick it up. Obviously it was intended for wearing because a chain, in the same shiny medium, rose seamlessly from the back of the angel's wings, just long enough to go around a neck. But wow! How could she wear something so precious? Perhaps mum wanted her to put it away somewhere; give it to dad for safekeeping? The letter would tell her. Tally left the pendant cradled in the velvet and continued reading:

"Jophiel is the angel of wisdom, understanding and judgement, and once you place the chain around your neck he will stay with you until it's time to move on – possibly to your own child, possibly to someone else. We do not choose, he does. Don't be afraid to wear it, Tally – wear it always. I don't know what it's made of. Maybe marble? I've never tried to find out; never saw the need. It is what it is, and it's very strong – it won't ever break, even though it looks so delicate.

This is my gift to you. It is priceless; let no one try to persuade you to sell it. You must give it freely to the next person, and you will know when.

And now, my darling, you must go to sleep. Yes, I asked Daddy to give you these things at bedtime, so I know you are already in bed. Put Jophiel around your neck, snuggle down and think of me - but with happiness.

Don't cry, my sweet girl. We will meet again.

Be happy, Tally, be happy.

I love you.

Mummy."

Tally couldn't obey her mother. She couldn't 'not cry'. The tears burned down her cheeks and her throat did that horrible achy thing it does when you try to weep quietly. It had been such a wretched day. She wanted her mum to be here, to hold her and make everything all right.

She looked at the pendant. How come she'd never seen mum wearing it?

Probably because how was anyone able to wear such a chunky thing? It would stick in her chest and keep her awake all night, she thought crossly, and she shoved it onto the bedside table. A precious object it may be, but it wasn't her mother. It wouldn't change anything. It might be priceless, but it could be worthless for all she cared at that moment. It wouldn't bring Mum back and that's all she wanted. She would figure it out in the morning. Right now she wanted only to cry herself to sleep.

She'd better put the lid on over the angel first though, she thought, and she reached out. Then she snatched her hand back. How odd! Hadn't his eyes been closed before? Now they looked very much open, like they were looking at her. Something compelled her to pick the pendant up.

Tally expected it to be cold, but it was warm, and although made of stone it didn't feel scratchy or hard. She studied the chain. It wasn't long enough to slip over her head, but there was a clasp, so tiny it was nearly invisible. She opened it easily though and put it round her neck.

There! She didn't even have to fumble - she did it up with no help from anyone and let the heavy, yet strangely light angel pendant fall onto her chest, just below her collarbone. Then she lay down and pulled the duvet over her ears.

She had got cold sitting up. She carried on weeping but did it quietly into the pillow. She didn't want Dad to hear her. He was probably dealing with his own sadness and wouldn't want to cope with hers too.

Eventually she got drowsy. The pendant seemed to nestle against her chest like a miniature hot water bottle. Then she had the strangest sensation, as if she were shrinking; getting smaller and smaller until she was no bigger than the tiny angel and he could stretch his huge wings and fold them all around her to warm, comfort and protect her. They were so soft, like duck-down or a fleecy blanket, yet strong enough to hold her weight as if she herself had become a feather. Her deep sadness lifted, and she allowed herself to sink into the downy depths of the angel's wings and drift gently off to sleep.

CHAPTER THREE

"I am Jophiel and I represent wisdom, understanding and judgement. I failed in my first task. I failed to prevent the firstborn man from murdering his brother and presuming he would escape punishment. So unwise. He showed no understanding, and he lacked judgement. All elements in my care. Everyone hears how the Lord banished him to the land of Nod.

No one ever asks what happened to me."

Tally didn't see much of her dad over the next few days. Apart from meals, he stayed in his study where she heard him talking on the phone, but never made out what he said. She was desperate to ask if he had thought about taking her with him but didn't dare, in case it reminded him she ought to be at school.

Instead, she kept herself busy around the house doing things that her mum would have done before she got ill. She washed up after meals, put the clothes in the washing machine (only making the mistake of putting something red in with light colours once) and did bits of cleaning, quietly so she didn't remind Dad of her presence. The rest of the time she fed and played with their two cats, Willow and Kayto, or curled up on the sofa with them to read a book. The hole in her life that her mum's absence had made was as big as the world, but she tried not to think about it. If she did she would hold the angel, and somehow everything became better.

On the fourth day her father called her into the study. She tried to stop her heart banging against her chest like a fly banging on a window and waited for him to speak.

"I've thought a lot about what you suggested, sweetheart," he began, "and spent the last few days finding out about home schooling and what it would involve."

She held her breath. It was impossible to tell which way this would go from her dad's face.

"So," he grinned, "I think we can make this work."

Tally screamed out loud and ran to throw her arms round her father. "Honestly?" she cried. "I don't have to go back to school, and we'll stay together?"

"Honestly," he promised. "And I must tell you, it's quite a relief for me too! I didn't quite know how I was going to drag myself away from you." He squeezed her hard before holding her away from him and putting on a stern face. "But you will have to go back sometimes for assessments and to sit exams. And you will have to work hard. We can get the courses online and most of it will be doable on the laptop. However, if you don't keep up with the lessons - and a lot of it will be up to you to do on your own - then the agreement ends, and you will go to boarding school. We'll find a different one if you're unhappy at the Academy, but – I repeat – you will go if I'm not satisfied that you're keeping up your end of the bargain."

"I promise," Tally breathed, "to do everything you want and make you proud of me."

Dad ruffled her silky blond hair (she hated that, but never had the heart to ask him not to do it) and then hugged her again. "And I've got some more news. Everything's happening so quickly!" He brushed his hand over his eyes. "It wasn't what I had in mind, but I've had a call from a colleague of mine in India. Apparently he's got a big project on now and wants me to help a bit in the hospital. He's asked me to go immediately. So, unless you have any objections, that's our first destination. I've booked the tickets and we leave the day after tomorrow."

Tally squealed. "WHAT? So soon?" She couldn't believe her luck. "Wow, you're amazing!"

Then her face clouded over, and she slumped down into a chair. "But what about this house? What about Willow and Kayto?" She realised that she'd only been thinking about herself. How could she have forgotten about the cats? Kayto pushed open the study door at that moment and came rubbing round her legs, meowing for attention. She patted her knee, and he jumped up for her to wrap her arms around his warm body and bury her cheek in his fur.

"Well, that's already sorted too." Dad sounded pleased. "Aunt Jayne did suggest at the funeral that she come and stay with us, to help take care of you and the house. So, I've spoken to her, and she has agreed to move in and manage everything while we're away."

Tally was ecstatic. Perfect! The cats adored Dad's sister Jayne, so much so that Tally sometimes felt quite jealous of the way they attached themselves to her whenever she visited. But now Tally was really glad. The cats would be totally happy, and she needn't worry about them at all.

She would have to go into school and collect her belongings, she thought smugly. Oh, she couldn't wait to brag to those vile girls that she was going to India; to travel instead of attend stinking school. And while they were bogged down in classrooms with boring lessons, or having to play games in the rain, she would be swanning about in the sunshine learning things they couldn't even imagine in their dreams. She would make them so envious! She would really rub it in, especially to that Elyssia who acted as if she was the queen of the class. Tally would show her –

Suddenly a deluge of icy water sloshed over Tally's head, soaking her hair, and dripping into her eyes. As she cried out loud and her body jerked with the shock, Kayto leapt off her lap as if something had stung him. She put up her hands to push her wet hair out of her face... but it was dry. Yet she had felt the water. How could that be? She looked at her knees; also dry. Kayto sat on the carpet washing his paws, but only out of indignation at her treatment. He didn't have a drop on him either.

Dad looked at her quizzically. "You OK?"

Tally opened her mouth to tell him what had happened, but no words came out. Instead she nodded, and he turned back to his computer. Something moved against Tally's chest. She tugged the neck of her sweatshirt out to peer down at the angel pendant which had twisted and seemed to float away from her body.

The angel's head was turned towards her and his eyes bored into her own. Tally swallowed nervously. Jophiel was looking at her with sadness tinged with rebuke. It sort of reminded her of her mum when she was disappointed in something Tally had done. But how? She must be imagining it! A heavy lump of stone couldn't float like that.

She let her top fall back into place and murmured an excuse to her dad about going to her room.

He nodded. "We'll work out the details later, sweetheart. I just need to deal with a few emails. Why don't you make us a sandwich and we'll talk about our plans over lunch?"

Tally stepped past Kayto and crept out.

CHAPTER FOUR

"The creator made an example of me. Other angels failed in their tasks (where's perfection nowadays? Does peace abound?) but their omissions were slow to manifest. Because my lapse in judgement allowed the Very First Crime, He cast me out from Heaven. If not for the intervention of my brother Sarathiel, Angel of discipline and penance, I would have joined the ranks of the Fallen like Harut or Azazel and the notorious Lucifer."

As soon as she reached the sanctuary of her room, Tally tore off her sweatshirt and scrutinised the angel pendant in the mirror. Once again, his eyes were shut. There was no hint that, just a few minutes ago, he had been staring at her.

She must be going mad. There was no other explanation. It must be the excitement causing her to hallucinate. She cradled the tiny angel in her hand and stared at it.

"Jophiel?" she whispered, feeling silly.

No way! His minuscule eyes slowly opened and gazed into her own again. Somehow, although he was only the size of her thumb, with eyes mere pinpricks, Tally could see them as if they were as big as her own. In fact, the angel seemed to fill the room. When he spoke, his voice came from all around, ringing like a gong.

"Tally!"

With a strangled cry, Tally dropped the pendant immediately, but it made no difference. The angel remained. He was inside her head; he was filling the room; he was standing in front of her like a featureless mist and yet swinging from the chain on her chest.

She stumbled backwards, terrified. She wanted to run out of the room and into the garden and never stop running.

"Do not be afraid!" The angel spoke again, and instantly Tally wanted to stay exactly where she was and talk to this extraordinary apparition. Her terror had vanished, seemingly along with her voice. She opened and closed her mouth a few times before she finally squeaked, "What's happening?"

The angel smiled, and then Tally thought she would explode with happiness. It was a happiness that made even Christmas morning seem dull. It bubbled up from inside her and made her want to sing, laugh and cry all at the same time. She wanted to fling her arms wide and hug the nearest person. Luckily, she realised when she calmed down a bit, there was no one near, because they'd be carting her off to an asylum otherwise.

Jophiel, his face neither young nor old, just kind and beaming, seemed to be waiting for her to speak. So, once she'd stopped reeling, she stammered, "Did you do that? Did you nearly drown me with cold water?"

"I did." He spoke gravely. "Your thoughts about your school mates were unworthy of you."

"But they're always horrible to me," Tally protested. "You don't know what it's been like. They're so mean. Why shouldn't I get my own back?"

"I do know, my child. But they have reasons for being the way they are. You must let them forge their own path, and you must forge yours. If you act the same way, then you are no better than they are."

"Do you know all my thoughts?" Tally whispered, a feeling of horror making her scalp prickle. "Because that's a bit creepy." In fact, if that was the case, she might have to ditch the pendant. She narrowed her eyes while she waited for Jophiel's answer.

"No," he replied. "Do not be afraid. Normally, unless you are in mortal danger, I can only enter your thoughts if you ask me to listen." He held up his hand as if making a vow. "I give you my word - and an angel cannot break his word - that I will only listen if you invite me by saying 'Jophiel, hear me'. Does that reassure you?"

Tally nodded cautiously, until the thought occurred to her, "Why did you listen before, then?"

"Actually, I was looking for a way to approach you. But then your mind filled so much with negativity and hate, I had to intervene. You judged your classmates without recognising their motivation. One day you will understand."

Tally frowned. "I want to understand now," she insisted, welling up with the familiar impatience that had often caused her mum to tease her. She completely ignored the bizarre fact that, standing in the middle of her bedroom, she was talking to an *angel* as comfortably as she talked to Willow or Kayto. How had that happened so quickly? It must be him. He must be making her feel like that. She waited for his answer.

"Very well." He steepled his fingers together and stared into the depths of her eyes. "With regards to your friend, Elyssia…"

"She's not my *friend*. She hates me. You should see the looks she gives me when we get exam results and I've come top."

"And what do you do?"

"Well," Tally said defiantly, "I try to stare her down. You know, show her I'm better than her." As soon as she said it, she was ashamed. She knew it was wrong, but it was out there now.

The angel's smile was gentle. "And do you think that behaving meanly or having spiteful thoughts makes you better than your classmates?"

"No, of course I don't," Tally mumbled, "but what *should* I do?"

"Perhaps if you smiled at her and made light of your own success, praising hers, she would feel different about

37

herself, and you. You could show her that you would rather be her friend than get high exam results."

Tally lowered her head. Maybe she hadn't tried hard enough. Maybe some of it was her fault that she had no friends. She'd never thought of it like that.

"Well, it's too late now, isn't it?" she muttered, gazing at her feet. "I won't be going back."

"No, but you can be kind when you go to collect your belongings. And you can try to think kindly of others generally. People are not always what they seem, and everyone carries their own burden."

Dejected, Tally sneaked a glance at the angel, worried he would be scowling. But his gentle smile made her feel like she could fly to the rooftops and back.

At that moment Dad's footsteps sounded on the stairs and the angel disappeared.

Dad appeared in her doorway. "I thought you were going to make us sandwiches," he chided good-humouredly. "It's well past lunchtime!"

Tally looked at the little clock on her bedside table. It was nearly two o'clock. But she'd only come upstairs minutes ago - where had all that time gone? She knew instinctively that her father hadn't seen Jophiel. Tally could still feel the angel's presence, though much diminished, but he no longer filled the room. He just continued to be there, warming her heart.

Immediately after lunch, Tally raced upstairs. She needed to start packing if they were leaving the day after tomorrow. She'd never packed a case all on her own. She remembered the trip they had all made to Cornwall last summer when Mum had let her help with the suitcases. "That's the best way to learn," Mum had said.

Tally felt the tears threaten. "Don't think, don't think," she said aloud. "I wonder if Jophiel is still here?" She made a sweep of the room. A moment ago it had been empty, but now the angel was floating by the window, his gigantic wings brushing the ceiling and his white robes rippling. Tally had to look up to his face. She couldn't make out the features clearly. He shimmered so brightly, she had to lower her gaze.

"I am always with you," was his reply. "I am bound to the pendant, not the last place in which you saw me."

"Sorry," Tally muttered. "I just didn't know whether you were here all the time or if I had to call you."

"But you did call me. You said my name out loud. Did you want something in particular?"

How could she explain? She just wanted to know he was there. He made her want to sing! Even dance! How could she tell him that looking at him was like looking at her mum, her dad, her cats – every single thing that she'd ever loved? Like looking at love itself! No, she couldn't say any of those things, because she was also a teeny weeny bit scared of him.

"N-no. Nothing really," she stammered, and she bent to drag her suitcase from under her bed. Better to get on with it and show Dad she could be grown up.

She frowned at her wardrobe. What should she take? It would be hot in India so that was a bonus – she wouldn't need winter clothes and summer ones took up much less space. She'd be able to take more.

Tally started dumping her clothes on the bed until there wasn't an inch of duvet visible. When she couldn't think of anything else she might need, she began putting things in the case, rolling and folding, layering and piling, the way Mum had shown her. Then stuffing and pushing and getting extremely cross when the lid wouldn't close. She tried again. And again. Why, oh why couldn't she fit everything in? Almost screaming with frustration, she flung the contents of the case onto the floor.

Then she looked round furtively. Was that angel watching her bad behaviour?

Yes, he was! And... he was laughing at her. Her temper overflowed.

"Why are you laughing at me? Don't laugh!" Tally shouted. "I hate packing. I can't fit everything in. I don't want to go!"

Jophiel continued to smile.

"Don't look at me like that! Why don't you do something to help?"

"I am not a genie, Tally," the angel retorted, his smile going out like a light. "I don't grant wishes or do magic tricks." His tone softened. "I am here to guide you, child. So, let me help you help yourself; get a pin."

"What sort of pin?"

"Just a dressmaker's pin."

"Do I look like someone who makes their own clothes?" Tally snapped back, still smarting.

"Maybe not." Jophiel smiled. "But your mother used to, and there are plenty in her sewing drawer."

As soon as he mentioned her mum, Tally wilted. She was behaving atrociously and she knew it. Without another word she went to the spare bedroom where her mum had kept her sewing things and found a box of pins. There were one or two rather special ones with round, coloured heads, and she chose one with a red blob on the top. She held it up for Jophiel's inspection.

"That will do nicely," he said. "Now lay it against your finger very gently and let all your anger flow into the metal. Don't prick yourself, keep it flat."

Tally had already replaced her anger with curiosity. But she did as he asked.

How weird was that? It *was* as if all her frustration was flowing out of her - and into the little red topped pin. She held it a little longer. She felt much better.

"Now what?" she asked.

"Now, find the corner of a seam somewhere on your clothes. Somewhere where the fabric is a bit thick."

Tally fingered along the collar of her sweatshirt until she could feel the thick corner part. Jophiel nodded his approval.

"Perfect," he agreed. "Now, slide the pin into the seam. The head will stop it disappearing, the fabric will prevent it pricking you."

She obeyed, and the pin rested harmlessly along the length of the seam.

"Now, you always have it with you," he continued. "And whenever you feel angry and frustrated, you can channel it all into the metal. It's also quite useful if you ever need to pin anything," he finished gravely.

Tally wasn't sure whether to laugh or cry. She did feel better. Jophiel did that to her.

"And I need to remember to transfer it onto whatever I'm wearing at the time," she said dryly, and she began to rescue the clothes that she had scattered all over the floor.

"Well, there is that," Jophiel agreed. "Last time I recommended someone do this, they had one single overcoat that they wore all the time. It was so much simpler. Nowadays people have too many clothes."

"Well, I've certainly got too many to fit into this suitcase," Tally countered good-humouredly, and she began to choose things to put back in the drawers. She didn't need all that stuff anyway. On second thoughts – she took them out of the drawers again – they probably wouldn't fit her by the time she got back. "They can all go to the charity shop," she declared.

Jophiel beamed his approval.

CHAPTER FIVE

"Wandering the earth in human form was dangerous. I had nowhere to sustain my vigour. I wafted and accomplished little with diminishing strength. Malevolent forces, which spring from the sins of mankind (and that fiery place that none of us likes to mention) hunted me, intent on my destruction. I was vulnerable to attack from fiends and demons, exposed to the gaze of the Creator.

I needed to hide."

On the morning of departure Tally and her dad checked the house once more, then, satisfied they had forgotten nothing, said goodbye to Aunt Jayne, Willow and Kayto and drove away in a taxi.

The bustle of the airport swirled around Tally like a river.

"Where do we go? What do we do?" she asked.

Dad smiled and handed her a piece of paper with the flight number written on it. "We go over to that huge monitor," he pointed ahead, "and we look for our flight there. That will tell us which desk number we need for check-in and where to leave our cases."

She took the paper from her dad's hand and scanned the list of all the flights leaving in the next few hours.

"Wait for the page to change," Dad explained. "There are so many flights. They don't all fit at once."

At last, Tally spotted it. "D 25-30," she called out. But Dad was already walking away, towards the section with a huge letter D in lights overhead. She hurried after him.

The queue was short and as there were five check-in desks for their flight they didn't have to wait long.

Dad handed the passports to the lady behind the counter. Tally stared at her. She looked more like a supermodel than an airline clerk. And was that really the uniform? That rich cream and orange sari looked so awesome. Tally wished she had clothes like that; and hair that colour. She would swap her own so-blond-it-was-almost-white locks for brunette any day.

"Good morning, Mr Carter, Miss Carter," said the lady, as she read the names on the passports.

"He's a doctor really," Tally couldn't stop herself from explaining.

"Natalie!" Dad remonstrated.

"Then he must be a surgeon," smiled the lady. Tally felt robbed. She loved explaining to people why consultant surgeons are Mr instead of Doctor. It's an old tradition. But this lady knew.

Dad looked embarrassed. "I'm so sorry," he murmured, as he took the passports and boarding cards.

"Not at all." The woman smiled. "The security and departure gates are to your right and you'll be boarding at 11. Plenty of time to go shopping." She winked at Tally. "Have a pleasant flight!"

"Tal, you mustn't go around telling everyone I'm a doctor," Dad scolded as they walked towards the security gates. "Otherwise everyone will be telling me about their migraines and showing me their rashes."

Tally laughed and strode on ahead, eager to get to the next phase of her adventure.

As they came out of security and into the departure lounge, her excitement levels soared again. It looked like a huge shopping mall with stores, bars and cafés. Tally dragged her dad from one to another, scrutinising every shelf of glittery jewellery, bright clothes and smart leather shoes; then every stand with tiny kettles, miniature irons, earphones and neck pillows.

The two hours whizzed by, and long before she had had enough Dad steered her towards the departure gate and onto the plane.

"Now," he said, as he showed her how to buckle her seat belt. "It's a school day. So, don't think you're going to recline your seat and watch back-to-back movies."

Tally squashed the impulse to argue. She had promised, and she had to show that she could keep her word. Meekly she accepted the wodge of papers and exercise books that Dad took out of his backpack.

"You can see us take off first," he capitulated. "There's plenty of time for study. It will take us over eight hours to fly to New Delhi - that's longer than a typical school day! So, work hard and you *may* have time for a movie."

Tally nodded, then concentrated on the cabin crew making their safety demonstration. Maybe she could be a flight attendant? It looked amazing. She didn't understand why some people took no notice. Imagine going to the theatre and not bothering to watch the performers? It would drive her nuts. Perhaps she wouldn't be a flight attendant.

Take-off was amazing! Tally stared out of the window at the tarmac angling away from her as the plane rose into the air. Soon they were right in the middle of the clouds, and seconds later, above them. It was like flying over an endless, white, billowy duvet.

Reluctantly she turned her back on the incredible view and arranged her schoolbooks on the drop-down table. School work sucked, but if she had to do it, then this was the place. It was like she was in her own little world, the thrum of the plane's engines creating a comforting background sound. But best of all, the attendants just kept bringing drinks and snacks without her even asking. She finished the day's assignments in no time.

Then lunch came, all in little dishes and with a miniature salt and pepper pot. Could she keep that? Tally wondered. After Dad had looked over her work and approved, he let her turn on her personal TV screen and lose herself in the latest movie. Tally reclined her seat as much as it would go, propped a pillow under her head, wrapped herself in a blanket and basked. She never wanted the flight to end!

And all the time Tally was conscious of the warm spot on her chest where the angel rested. It had become a habit to hold on to it when she had nothing else to do with her hands. She still marvelled at the warmth and softness of the stone. It was like a furry kitten rather than a lump of sculpted marble.

Did Jophiel exist? she mused, gently caressing the effigy. *Had* she talked to an angel in her bedroom? Or had she imagined it? Come to think of it, she couldn't even say what colour his eyes were, nor his skin (if he even had skin). She was pretty sure he didn't have a beard – or did he?

One thing Tally did know, she mustn't call him now because he'd warned her never to talk aloud to him when anyone else was around. Not even her dad.

But hang on; he had said he would speak to her in her mind if she gave him permission.

Timidly, she tried the phrase he had given her. *"Jophiel, hear me."*

"I am here, my child," he replied.

Oh, wow! It *was* real.

"Isn't this fantastic?" she enthused.

"What?" came his acerbic reply.

"Flying!"

She felt the pendant at her throat quiver. No way! Did he just shudder? *"You can't be scared,"* she laughed. *"Angels can't be afraid of flying, surely?"*

"No," he bristled. *"I do not fear* flying. *It's these unnatural birds that I dislike. And not on my behalf, but for the fragile human life forms that they carry. If the Creator had wanted Man to fly, he would have given him wings."*

Tally giggled out loud, then had to pretend she'd seen something funny on the screen when her dad raised his eyebrows.

"*Well, what about cars then? Should he have given us wheels instead of feet?*" Tally continued the mental conversation.

"*That's different,*" Jophiel huffed. "*Cars are an adaptation of the donkey. A natural progression.*"

"*They're not as safe as planes though, I read,*" insisted Tally. "*Statistics say...*"

"*I know, I know,*" he interrupted. "*People say it all the time. I merely tremble for your fragility. I shall rest in my image. Tell me when we get there.*"

He'd gone. The space in her head was lonely without him. So, Tally comforted herself by clutching the pendant in her hand for the rest of the trip.

Before she knew it, they were landing in New Delhi.

CHAPTER SIX

"Sarathiel led me to caves on Mt Sinai, in Egypt. Heavenly forces abounded there, and I absorbed energy from the rock itself. I became strong and capable of taking form. I desired to return to my work, but was reliant on the secrecy of the cave."

As they exited the airport Tally was very aware that she was no longer in England. Absolutely nothing was the same. It wasn't only the heat, which was weird enough in the early hours of the morning, but the noises, the smells and the colours. She was almost blinded by the oranges, blues and yellows of people's clothes that stood in vivid contrast to the black sky. And the rubbish! She wrinkled her nose at the strong odour of litter that was hanging in the air.

A guide ushered them to a 4x4 car and Tally was thankful for the sanctuary; and for the garland of sweet-smelling petals that he ceremoniously placed round their necks to welcome them to India. What a relief to get out of the noise. The air-conditioning meant they were able to keep the windows shut, and she could press her nose against the glass to peer at the surrounding scenes in comfort.

Was it always this busy at half-past one in the morning? At home it would only be about 8 pm (Tally had a moment's nostalgia while she wondered what Aunt Jayne and the cats were doing) but did no one go to bed here?

Then she looked a bit closer at the hundreds of boxes and tarpaulins scattered along the roads. Were there feet sticking out of that one? And that one? Amazed, she realised that every box or tarpaulin housed at least one person. Of course, she'd seen homeless people in England, but never so many in one place. Gazing around the comfortable car and all their luggage piled up in the boot, she felt embarrassed. She had so much. These people had their entire home in a cardboard box.

She pulled on her dad's sleeve and pointed at some makeshift dwellings under a bridge. "What can we do?" she agonised. "Can we sell some stuff and give them some money?"

Dad hugged her, kissing the top of her head. "Even if we sold every single thing that we have, and threw the money out into the street, it wouldn't make any difference, sweetheart. There are so many poor people in the world. We must do what we can in other ways."

"Like what?" Tally queried, watching a young mother settle her baby on the ground between herself and her husband.

"Well," Dad continued, "I'm doing a bit in the hospital. I know children start learning English here very young. Maybe you could ask at local schools if they have any reading projects you could get involved with, if you're interested?"

Tally nodded. She was too tired to think about how she'd do that right now. It was a relief when they got to their hotel, had some divine tasting chicken with naan bread, and went to bed.

In the daylight New Delhi was busier than London at rush hour – and a whole lot hotter. Tally would have liked to have explored it, but they weren't staying. Their destination, and the location of Dad's friend, was Agra, home of the Taj Mahal. She had seen loads of photos of it but hadn't really got excited. After all, it was just a building, wasn't it? In fact, it was just a building around a coffin, not even a house. Dad had made her read about it. Apparently, some Emperor called Shah Jahan had built it for the body of his favourite wife.

A whole building for a dead body! And yet people lived
in cardboard boxes and under tarpaulins. It was heart-
breaking. Tally thought about it constantly as they waited
for their train in New Delhi station.

Never had she experienced a station like the one at
Delhi. She vowed that she wouldn't complain about
English stations again. She had a moment's fear that she
had seen the last of her suitcase as a porter whisked it
away, balancing it on his head. She lost sight of him
amongst so many people, cars, bikes and motorbikes, all
milling about in what seemed utter confusion. And there
were as many animals as people – dogs and goats mainly.
Even a cow wandered in. Everyone steered around it, no
one shooed it out, even when it left a massive cow pat on
the floor.

"Cows are sacred," Dad explained as Tally stared in
amazement. "They can go where they like, and no one will
send them away."

"What about goats?" asked Tally, pointing to one munching happily on some bits of green salad leaves half-buried under a pile of garbage in a corner.

Dad smiled and shook his head. "No, they're not sacred, but animals are well treated here."

Dogs lay sleeping on the stairs and Tally saw how people stepped round them or over them, accepting them as part of the landscape. One, lying quite near to where she stood, was covered in tiny bits of blossom that had blown off a nearby tree. He wasn't bothered in the slightest. At first, she worried that he was dead, till he opened one eye to check he wasn't missing a titbit from the people sitting on the platform. There were few chairs, so people hunkered down on the floor, amongst the litter and muck. How the women kept their saris so spotlessly clean and elegant looking was beyond Tally. She was sweaty and dusty in her cut-off jeans and T-shirt. In fact, she felt scruffy compared to all the exquisite women and girls in their silks and jewellery. They didn't even look warm, never mind hot.

While they waited, trains were waved through by a man brandishing what seemed to be a piece of rag on a broom handle. People hung out of windows and doors or even sat on the roofs. Tally's eyes became sore and gritty from the scorching dirty air.

Eventually their train arrived, and they found their pre-booked seats in a small first-class compartment. OK, so it wasn't the Orient Express (which she'd seen once in a film), but the tatty plastic seats surprised her. As did the miniscule table, not even big enough for a laptop, by a filthy window. If these were the best seats on the train, she wondered what the other carriages were like.

The last straw came when Dad opened the picnic the hotel had given them. He set it out on the table and instantly tiny cockroaches came swarming out from behind the panelling and scuttled towards the food.

"No," Tally shrieked, leaping up from her seat and bolting for the door. While Dad scooped up their picnic and re-positioned it on the top of his backpack on the seat, she silently called for her angel.

"Jophiel, hear me."

"What is wrong, what has happened?" he demanded. She nodded to the cockroaches.

"Is that all?" he chuckled. *"I thought you had been attacked by demons. Cockroaches are merely beings such as yourself. They want to eat the food, not you."*

"I don't care – get rid of them!" Tally shouted, forgetting that she wasn't supposed to talk to Jophiel in public.

In a tone that dripped boredom, the angel reminded her that he wasn't a genie, and she should channel her fear into the pin.

Luckily, Dad showed no surprise at her words.

"Sweetheart, look. They're going now that I've moved the food," he soothed.

Tally sat down again as near to the corridor door as possible. Then pressed her finger along the pin while muttering, "I hate all this litter and filth," in a voice just loud enough for her father to hear. He grinned at her and she tucked into her sandwiches, keeping a sharp look-out for marauding cockroaches.

She felt better after using her pin, so much better that she scolded herself for being so precious. She was here to experience new things, wasn't she? What's the point of travelling the world to see what's different, then complaining when it's not the same?

Afterwards she helped Dad secure the leftovers. The insects hadn't ventured further than the walls of the train and had all disappeared again, but Tally wasn't taking any chances. When they arrived in Agra, she checked every inch of her backpack before picking it up and hoisting it onto her shoulders. Thank goodness the journey had only been a couple of hours and they hadn't had to sleep on the train. She would never have been able to close her eyes.

"Well, we would have slept with our heads towards the corridor," mused Dad when she shared this with him. "I doubt they would have been interested in our feet."

During the taxi ride to the house that Dad's friend had rented for them, Tally got the impression that Agra was shabbier than New Delhi. The buildings were older, less well cared for, and there weren't as many high-rise offices or apartments. The streets seemed dustier too, but it was equally busy. She began to feel apprehensive about their new home.

So when they drew up outside a tidy, white painted building which had a wall all around and a small garden, Tally sighed with relief. Trees heavy with flowers surrounded the house, which smelled clean and fresh inside. They had a bedroom each with a giant wooden ceiling fan lazily stirring the air. The bathroom was small, but clean and modern. There was a kitchen, a dining room, and a lounge with TV. White linen, that had clearly been washed that day, covered heavy, dark wood furniture that

looked like it would hurt if you stubbed your toe on it.
Tally breathed in the soapy freshness of the room.
Everything was pristine.

Dad's friend, Raj, met them at the door and placed
garlands of flowers round their necks, like the guide in
Delhi had done. Slightly taller than her dad but just as
slim, Raj looked as if he'd walked out of a launderette. His
trousers were pressed into razor sharp creases and his
shirt almost crackled with starch. Even his immaculately
clipped beard and short black hair looked ironed.

"Very, very welcome," he beamed, shaking Dad's hand
vigorously and kissing Tally's. She'd never had her hand
kissed before and she blushed. It made her feel like a
princess, though even more conscious of her dirty,
crumpled clothes next to this man.

Raj introduced them to Abha, the lady who would cook,
clean and do shopping for them. Instead of the traditional
sari, she was wearing a green silk tunic and matching
trousers. Tally had noticed a lot of the younger women in

the streets dressed like that. She thought how great they looked on Abha, whose eyes expressed the warmest welcome before she spoke. And her English was fantastic!

"Sorry I can't stop to help you unpack, but I need to get home and cook for my own family. I'll see you tomorrow. I've left everything you should need in the kitchen and food is cooked and waiting in the fridge." And she left with a cheery wave.

Leaving Dad talking to Raj, Tally dragged their suitcases into their respective bedrooms. Back in her own room, she kicked off her shoes to feel the exquisite coolness of the tiled floor and began unpacking. She soon filled the numerous cupboards and wondered what to do next. She could hear Raj telling her Dad about where to find the best places to eat, what time to visit the Taj Mahal and how to get to the clinic, which led them onto medical stuff. Nothing Tally could get involved with, so, fed up with being inside, she left them to their conversation and ventured out into the garden.

"Can you smell that, Jophiel?" Tally took great breaths of the perfumed air. "It's coming off the trees – those flowers are unbelievable."

She held the pendant in front of her, but the angel had left it and walked beside her. Well, floated really, Tally thought as she looked up at him. His slightly see-through form seemed to glide with none of the effort a human would need.

"Ah," Jophiel murmured. "I don't actually inhale as you do, child, but I am perfectly aware of the power of the scent."

"What do you mean?" Tally frowned.

"Well, for me it exists. I don't breathe it in through my nose, but I am aware of it."

"That's weird," Tally giggled, pushing her face into the branches of a bougainvillea plant loaded with bright pink flowers.

"Are you talking to me?" came a voice from within the bush, causing Tally to jump backwards with a little squeal.

Jophiel swirled into a mist and poured himself into the pendant; *exactly* like a genie into a lamp, despite his protests.

Tally looked around. Surely the plant wasn't speaking? Though after Jophiel, anything was possible.

But no, as she peered closer, she realised that the bougainvillea grew up a fence covering a gate-sized gap in the wall. She parted the branches and tumbling flowers to see a tall Indian boy, standing on the other side grinning at her. He looked to be a couple of years older than Tally, with glossy black hair and skin the colour of melted chocolate. His dark eyes sparkled at her.

"How do you do," he said formally, despite his cheeky smile. "I am called Balvan. I saw you arrive earlier. I wanted to meet you because I have never seen hair that colour before, except on TV. It is very amazing."

Tally made the gap bigger to get a better look at her admirer. "I'm Tally. I only came to India yesterday – well, we, I mean. My dad and me. Do you live near here?"

"Around the corner." Balvan pointed along the dusty street. "My parents have a silk shop. They make saris, salwar kemees, dhotis, anything you want. Come and visit!"

"Whoa!" Tally laughed. "What are they? I mean, I know what a sari is, but the others?"

"Salwar kemees are the tunics and trousers that you see many ladies and girls wearing. More comfortable for in the city than saris. Dhotis are the cloths that men wear when they are not wearing trousers."

Tally noticed that Balvan was wearing cotton trousers and a Manchester United football shirt, but she had seen a lot of men in what seemed to be a sheet tucked round their middles and reaching to their knees. So – dhotis! That would be a great snippet to drop into conversation and impress Dad.

"Would you like to come to our shop?" the boy continued. "My little sister would be delighted to see your white hair and my mother would be happy to sew some salwar kemees for you. You would be more comfortable," he added, gesturing to her travel worn jeans and t-shirt with a delicate, long-fingered hand.

Tally's cheeks flamed. "Well, I can't simply walk out of the garden. I'd have to go and ask my dad first."

Balvan leaned over the fence to peer round the garden. "Of course, you must. But you were talking to someone just now. Was that not your father?"

At that moment, Dad called from the house.

"*That's* my Dad," Tally declared. "I must go." Then she blurted, "You could come in and meet him if you like?"

It would be good to make some friends, and she liked this boy, though they'd only exchanged a few words. He seemed fun. And he was fit! But no way Dad would let her go off on her own, or with anyone *he* hadn't met. So why not start immediately and introduce Balvan?

The boy's infectious smile reappeared. "Thank you for the honour," he beamed, and headed for the entrance to the garden.

CHAPTER SEVEN

"Sarathiel provided the solution. He brought to me a stone mason. A young man so talented he shaped rock to resemble a thing living. Sarathiel's plan was for him to carve a tiny piece of rock in my image, into which I would surrender my spirit and hide for eternity."

Tally met Balvan on the path and took him into the house.

Dad and Raj turned as she entered with her new friend, who put his hands together in front of his chest and said "Namaste, Uncles."

Tally's eyebrows shot up to her hairline. They weren't his uncles! Well, Raj might be, but her dad definitely wasn't.

Raj spotted her confusion and smiled. "Do not be alarmed! It is normal for young people to address older people as uncle and aunty, even complete strangers," he explained. He returned Balvan's greeting in the same manner, then said, "You are Balvan, aren't you? Son of Ashok Chabra?"

"Yes, Uncle, I am."

Raj turned to Dad. "I am acquainted with this boy's family. They are very esteemed." His next comment made Tally think he had been reading her mind. "If he and his sister were to befriend your daughter, it would be quite respectable. And desirable." He looked sideways at Dad and lowered his voice. "Bearing in mind what I was just telling you. He is old enough to be overlooked."

Tally looked from one to the other. "What's going on?" she asked.

Dad spoke to Raj. "We don't keep secrets and anyway, I'd far rather she is aware of the dangers." Then he addressed Tally. "Raj has just been telling me that, for a while now, children have been going missing. It's very serious, no one can find any trace of them."

Tally's mouth dropped open. "That's horrible," she whispered. "Do you mean children my age? How many? Am...am *I* in danger?"

Raj held up his hand. "You mustn't worry, Miss Tally, though you must be vigilant. Our police are taking this very seriously and they have put extra officers patrolling the streets. However, I am confident they will soon solve the mystery, and everything will get back to normal."

Balvan nodded in agreement, but Tally turned to her Dad for reassurance.

"I don't think you need to be scared, Tal," he said, though he looked sombre. "If Raj thinks the kidnappers will soon be caught, I'm sure it'll blow over. But you need to know there are dangers. You must never go out on your own, though I'd say that anyway. Everything is so new to both of us."

Tally hadn't intended going off on her own till she got used to things a bit, but Dad hadn't finished. "So don't be frightened, but don't leave the house without either me or Abha."

"Or me," piped up Balvan. "I'll be your tour guide. I know all the best places!"

"Don't you have to go to school?" Dad raised one eyebrow.

Balvan made a dismissive motion with his hand. "After school. And at the weekends," he continued hopefully. "And doesn't Tally have to go to school too?"

Dad explained about Tally's home schooling. "Anyway," he ruffled her hair fondly, "I'm giving her tomorrow off. We're going to do a bit of sightseeing. Take in the Taj Mahal."

"Oh Uncle, allow me to accompany you to see our precious Taj Mahal – in the morning, before school? I can show you the way, and I know the man on the ticket gate. We can get in before the queue."

"We had intended to go at dusk," Dad mused.

"Oh no, no, no. Please – dawn is much better. Like magic."

Tally held her breath, willing her dad to agree. It would be much more fun to go with Balvan.

Dad looked at Raj.

"Either time has its merits," he agreed. "And you can go more than once. I have a full day tomorrow, so I cannot take you. If the boy is willing, it would give you a chance to become acquainted with him." He looked fiercely at Balvan and spoke rapidly in their own language. Tally tried not to giggle as Balvan nodded his head vigorously. His expression alternated between worried and delighted, then worried again. She wished she understood what they were saying. Perhaps Jophiel did. She mustn't forget to ask him.

Eventually they decided that Balvan would meet them at 6 am with a taxi. Tally tried not to show her excitement as she said goodbye to him and Raj.

"Right!" Dad rubbed his hands together. "Eat, unpack, then sleep!"

Except that sleep was the last thing on Tally's mind. The moment she was alone in her room, she pulled the pendant from under her top.

"Jophiel!" She struggled to keep her voice quiet, she was so excited. "Can you speak Hindi? What were Raj and Balvan saying? Can you tell me?"

Jophiel appeared, sitting on the edge of the chest of drawers. "Just the usual adult to young person warnings about looking after you and your father. About politeness, respect. It was nothing mysterious."

"You do speak Hindi!" Tally squeaked. "How useful is that? When did you learn? Have you been here before?"

Jophiel sighed. "I understand every language, child. I don't need to learn them. They just are. And I have been everywhere."

Oh, there was so much to learn about him. Tally opened her mouth to ask another question, but Dad called across the hall. "Go to bed, Tal."

When the alarm went off the next morning, Tally was fast asleep and didn't want to drag herself from her dreams. Until she remembered the reason for the early start. Then she bounced out of bed and, after a quick shower, pulled on the shortest shorts and tiniest top that she had in her cupboards. India felt too hot for clothes! It was already warm, and she felt the fresh perspiration running down her back and starting to form a damp patch on her back.

Her excitement at seeing Balvan again was brimming over. So it was like a slap in the face when he frowned as she and her dad approached the taxi half an hour later.

"What's wrong?" she demanded.

"Um, it would be more respectful to our culture if you put on a long skirt, or long trousers, to visit Taj," he said hesitantly. "And covered your shoulders."

Her face burned. Why hadn't Jophiel warned her? What good was a guardian angel (as she liked to think of him) if he didn't guard her against mistakes?

"I'm too hot!" she fumed. "I don't have any long skirts and all my trousers are jeans. They're very thick." She threw herself onto the back seat of the taxi in a temper. Dad didn't follow. She hated the way he was standing outside the taxi, not saying a word but waiting for her to get out again and change. Nobody spoke, and she wanted to scream.

"Oh, all *right*." Tally gritted her teeth and dragged herself out of the taxi and into the house, where she ripped off her shorts and pulled on a pair of jeans. The steam of anger and humiliation rose off her like the vapour off a boiling pot. She didn't want to go to the Taj Mahal after all. She'd stay here and do her schoolwork. It would be far more interesting than some silly old building.

As she glared at her reflection in the mirror, she felt Jophiel's feather-soft wings envelop her. "Don't forget the pin," he reminded. For a few seconds she remained rebellious, but then she rescued it from the waistband of her shorts. She pressed it against her finger and exhaled.

That was better. Her frustration drained into the metal, leaving her calm and able to see what an idiot she'd been. She pushed it into the seam of her jeans.

Two minutes later she was getting back into the taxi, ashamed of her outburst. Should she say sorry? She didn't want Balvan to think she was a spoilt child.

Before she could decide, Dad turned round in his seat with a huge grin on his face. "Balvan has come up with a plan," he enthused. "After we've been to the Taj, we'll go to his parents' shop and get you measured up for some of the tunics that the girls wear here."

"Salwar kemees," Balvan interrupted.

"Exactly! He says they're great things to wear in the heat."

Balvan nodded. "My mother will be so delighted to sew for you, Tally."

Tally blinked. She'd been so horrible. And she was being rewarded with new clothes? "Really?" she breathed. "That's awesome! I *love* those outfits."

Balvan beamed. "My mother will help you choose the colour that goes best with your hair," he said. "Aditi, my little sister, will believe you are a princess. She is only eight, and she longs to have white hair like yours. She has seen it in the Disney movies – you know – 'Freezing', or something like that."

Tally giggled. "'Frozen', you mean." She couldn't wait to meet Aditi.

Just then, through the car window, she spotted a beautiful white building in the middle of a lake. "Is that the Taj?" She pointed as they drove past.

Balvan shook his head. "Oh no, that is the Lakshmi Palace Hotel. It is being painted and made better – how do you say? Refurshed?"

"Refurbished," murmured Tally, mesmerised by the grand building. "What a lot of water! How deep is that lake?"

"It is a mystery," Balvan answered. "No one knows why there is so much water in the lake at this time of year. It should be almost dry, and yet the level never goes down. Nobody is ever seen working there either, but the building improves. Many people say it is haunted, and my father says no one will work there."

Tally gasped. "What if that's where they're hiding the kidnapped children? If no one will go there, it would be the perfect place."

Balvan scoffed. "Don't you think our police thought of that? They have been many times and checked. The owner lives there with a couple of servants. They found nothing else. And how would they get them there without someone seeing a boat going across?"

"Secret tunnels?"

He shook his head. "We have good police. They're all over this. And anyway, it's not only from Agra that children are disappearing – it's happening all over India. They must be taking them somewhere far away." The taxi stopped. "Now, we have arrived. We will get out here."

CHAPTER EIGHT

"I did not leap at this solution; the source of an Angel is infinite, vast, all powerful – how to contain it in a tiny pebble?"

Tally peeled herself off the taxi seat and jumped out, looking around with interest. But there was no sign of the historic monument from where they were standing, just hundreds of people milling around and a long queue snaking away from the entrance. They would have had a long wait if Balvan hadn't bought their tickets the evening before. He led them straight up to the front of the queue and with a nod from the gatekeeper, they entered.

They stepped out into the gardens and suddenly the Taj Mahal was in front of them. Time stopped as the white marble building shimmered and seemed to hover in the mist that rose off the river behind it. A lump formed in Tally's throat and tears stung her eyes. She snuck her hand into her dad's. He had tears in his eyes too. Neither of them spoke. Both knew the other was remembering Mum.

How could anything be so beautiful? A long rectangular pool led up to the mausoleum and its domed roofs reflected in the water.

Balvan touched her elbow. "Look at the four towers guarding the corners," he whispered. "Do you see how they lean outwards a bit?"

Tally nodded.

"They were designed like that purposefully," Balvan continued, "so that if they should ever fall, they wouldn't fall on the resting place of the emperor's favourite wife."

How romantic was that! Tally took a couple of quick snaps with her mobile, then Balvan led them down the well-tended (and miraculously clean) paths to the building.

"We can go inside, but we can't take photos," he explained. "And we have to be searched." He turned to Tally. "You will go in a different queue, for ladies. You don't mind, do you? You'll be OK!"

"Don't worry, it's fine," Tally assured him.

The queues moved quickly, so they were soon back together again with mobiles switched off as requested.

They followed the queues around the two tombs lying in the centre of the main chamber and protected by carved marble screens. Tally stared in awe at the mosaics, and was impressed when Balvan explained that each minute inlay was done by hand. It didn't seem possible – the gigantic building, walls, floors and ceilings, were all marble mosaic in thousands of different patterns.

It was spectacular, but after a while it got a teeny bit boring. There was nothing else in there. Just marble and two tombs. And none of it came close to the impact of that first moment.

Tally became impatient with the crowds and wanted to go outside again. On the way in she'd noticed a particular spot where people posed on a stone seat and took photos, looking as if they held the building in the palm of their hands. She wanted to have a go.

She tugged on her dad's sleeve. "Can I go outside and take some photos?" she pleaded. He was *so* engrossed in the tiles!

She could see he was about to refuse permission, but Balvan stepped in.

"We can go together," he offered. And Dad agreed.

Soon they joined the crowd by the seat. While Tally was waiting her turn, she gazed around. Near the steps leading to the platform were two men who seemed to be staring at her. They leaned nonchalantly against the wall and looked the other way when she looked back at them. But she was sure they'd been watching her.

She frowned but forgot about them as the seat became free.

"Quick," urged Balvan. "Before someone else gets in." He grabbed her phone and called directions as to how she should position her hand, so it looked like she was holding the mausoleum. Perhaps I'll be a model, Tally mused, as she posed this way and that.

Balvan handed the phone back, and they giggled at the results. Then Tally had a brainwave.

"Let's take a selfie," she cried, grabbing his arm, and pulling him round beside her. Instantly, she felt a pang of guilt. Maybe Balvan didn't know what a selfie was? But she needn't have worried.

He grinned and pulled out his own phone, saying, "Over here. This is the best place. I'll take one with mine too."

Tally checked the photos and looked up to make a comment to Balvan. There were those men again. She nudged Balvan and started to point them out, but by the time he turned round they'd disappeared into the crowd.

Tally was pleased that Balvan took her seriously. "What were they wearing?" he asked.

"One had a green T-shirt on with jeans. The other had a white shirt and a…" she searched for the word she'd learned last night, "dhoti," she finished.

Balvan shot her an admiring look. "Stay right here," he commanded. "I'll have a quick look round." And he dived into the crowds.

Even though she was surrounded by people, Tally was nervous waiting on her own. She kept thinking about what Dad had said last night and she held onto her pendant for comfort. Did Jophiel have the power to protect her from danger? Before she could invite him into her mind to ask him, Balvan came back. He shook his head.

"No sign. I'm sure it was nothing."

Tally wasn't so sure, but at that moment her father joined them, and she showed him her photos.

"Can I get a souvenir, Dad?" Tally asked, gazing around. "Do they have a gift shop?"

Balvan shouted with laughter. "Only about five hundred," he chortled. "As soon as we go outside the gates, we'll be mobbed by people selling souvenirs."

Tally frowned. "I'd like something to remember today," she said. "But how will I choose?"

"I know someone who makes the souvenirs himself," Balvan suggested. "Not these cheap factory ones. It won't be expensive, and it'll be handmade." He directed an enquiring gaze at Tally's dad.

"Lead the way!" Dad grinned.

As they exited the Taj, Tally took her dad's hand while Balvan scouted round for his friend. How he found him amongst the hordes of sellers Tally couldn't imagine, but he was back within minutes.

The seller had a selection of tiny replicas of the Taj. He'd carved them out of marble, and Tally loved them. She was amazed at how clever he was. But what made them perfect was that the stone reminded her of her angel pendant. She chose one the size of a matchbox. Perhaps Jophiel could live in it, she mused.

That night, Tally waited till she saw her dad's bedroom light go off before calling her angel. She couldn't wait to share the excitement of the day with him. Had he felt the magic of the Taj too?

She called softly into the darkness and Jophiel appeared at the end of her bed. His tall form glowed with the soft light that she could see when she looked at the pendant.

"I've had a brilliant day," Tally announced. "Did you see the Taj, Jophiel?"

She heard the smile in the angel's reply. "I did, child. It was nice to see it finished. Shah Jahan did well. He always was brilliant."

Tally's mouth dropped open. "You knew him? You were there when it was built?"

"Well, for some time, yes. The keeper of the pendant at that time was one of the architects. There were nine of them. He didn't last till the end, I'm afraid, so – neither did I."

Tally couldn't get her head round it. Jophiel was full of surprises.

"You could have been our guide," she said. "Is it true about the pillars?"

"Oh yes, Shah Jahan adored Mumtaz Mahal. He didn't want any harm to come to her in life or afterwards. But then, his own tomb is beside hers, so he may have been thinking of himself."

Tally guessed he was teasing. She was starting to feel sleepy so pulled the sheet up to her chin and settled her head into the pillow. "Dad would have built a Taj for Mum," she whispered, "if he could have."

"He did, child. It rests in his heart."

CHAPTER NINE

"But I could not hide in a cave forever. So, I agreed."

Over the next two days Tally and her dad got to grips with her study programme. They made a space for her to stack her books and set up Dad's laptop at one end of the kitchen table, which was cool because whenever Abha was there she would slip drinks and snacks to her.

Tally was determined to keep her promise and work hard. It wasn't difficult; she was used to studying on her own, and the way they set the courses up meant she only had to do a few hours in the mornings. Plus, there was no one to tell her off for taking time out to daydream.

Which was what she was doing while waiting for Dad to join her for breakfast the next morning when the doorbell rang. Abha went to answer it and returned carrying a package wrapped in brown paper.

"Your new outfit has arrived," she said.

"Already?" Tally couldn't believe Mrs Chabra had finished it. She'd only chosen the fabric the day before yesterday, and what fun that had been. It had been so difficult to decide between cream with turquoise, brown with exciting orange, lime green and pale blue, or that one that looked like a rainbow.

Little Aditi, before leaving for school, had pointed to a shimmering navy blue with cerise that Tally had admitted looked great with her hair.

She took the package from Abha.

"Try it on," the young woman urged.

Tally didn't need telling twice. She raced to her room and swapped her shorts and T-shirt for the soft silk.

It was so light, and although her arms were covered to her elbows she didn't feel in the slightest hot or restricted. She pulled on sandals and twirled in front of the full-length mirror. Then she tried the matching scarf, draping it round her neck or over her head as she had noticed the Indian girls do. Great for the sun, instead of a sunhat!

She felt like a Bollywood film star. Far too gorgeous to sit around and do schoolwork.

Piling her hair on top of her head, she struck a pose. Then she blushed. The pendant was lying on the top of her tunic, and Jophiel's tiny eye winked at her in the mirror.

Then he appeared in the room, sitting on the end of her bed.

"Vanity!" he admonished.

"I wasn't admiring *myself*," she protested, though she knew it was a fib. "I was admiring the *clothes*. And Mrs Chabra made them, not me. So, I was admiring *her*, really."

The angel gave her a look that told her he knew exactly what she'd been thinking.

Crestfallen, Tally stopped. "I've just realised – there's nowhere to put my pin. There are no seams thick enough to keep it from sticking in me. What should I do?"

"Look at my back," Jophiel instructed. Tally tried to peer round him, but his gigantic wings filled the room.

"On the pendant, silly," he chuckled. She picked it up and turned it over to peer at the reverse side. There was a ridge between the angel's wings. She'd never noticed that before. It looked like a quiver, empty of arrows. There was even a tiny hole in the top.

"Slip the pin in there," Jophiel said. "I will keep it safe for you and it will always be available."

Tally pushed the point into the hole and the pin came to rest with just the red bobble top showing like the hilt of a jewelled sword.

"Perfect!" she breathed. And with one last twirl, she returned to the kitchen to show Abha.

She wasn't there, but Dad was sitting at the table, drinking coffee.

"Wowee," he whistled.

Tally blushed and mumbled how comfortable it was. "I know it's not for every day, but I just had to try it on."

"And why not?" Dad smiled as he put down his cup. "Tally, I've had a call from Raj. He wants me to go to the clinic today. Will you be all right doing your schoolwork on your own? Abha will be here."

Tally nodded. "When I've finished can I go to show Mrs Chabra how well this fits?" She pointed to her new outfit.

"Not on your own," Dad reminded her.

"It's only round the corner, Dad. I'll be fine," she pleaded.

"No, Natalie." Dad insisted. Then he softened. "But you can go with Abha if she doesn't mind. Ask her when she comes in."

"OK. That's cool," Tally agreed and tucked into the pancake-like bread called 'dosa' that Abha had made. It tasted of cheese and was filled with a mixture of vegetables fragranced with spices. It was so different from the cereals or porridge that she had for breakfast in England, and a thousand times better.

Abha agreed to the plan, and after lunch they nipped round the corner to Balvan's house.

"Look, there's Aditi." Tally pointed to a little girl sitting in the doorway, playing with some remnants of fabric.

"That looks like off-cuts from your tunic," Abha laughed as the little girl went running to fetch her mum.

Mrs Chabra came out, all smiles, and with Abha translating exclaimed how lovely Tally looked. Aditi, who had been hovering behind her mum, came up for a closer look. Standing in front of Tally on tiptoes, she raised one small brown finger and touched the pendant of Jophiel. Tally smiled encouragingly at her, and Aditi took the angel in her hand.

"It's so beautiful," she whispered in perfect English.

Tally wished she could speak more than one language. "My mum gave it to me," she told the little girl. "It's very, very special." Aditi nodded and replaced the pendant just as her brother came out to join them.

"Suits you," Balvan said, nodding at her outfit, and Tally blushed.

"I hate to rush you, Tally," Abha said, "but I'm afraid I have to nip home and I must take you back first."

Tally tried to hide her disappointment. She didn't want to sit on her own at home, and she had a thousand questions she wanted to ask about life in India.

To her delight, Balvan stepped in. "Aunty," he said to Abha, "I know Aditi would like Tally to stay longer. Could I walk home with her later? I must go to the edge of town to pick up some sewing machine parts for my mum. I could show Tally around a bit."

Abha frowned and Tally crossed her fingers.

Then Abha smiled. "Well, your dad said he would be late, so I'm sure he would rather you had something to do. I'll see you later."

Aditi grabbed Tally's hand and pulled her through the shop into the shady living room of their house.

"Can I brush your hair?" Aditi pleaded.

Tally laughed. "I guess so," she agreed, and sat down on the tiled floor so the little girl could reach. Tally felt like a proper big sister as the younger girl brushed and plaited her long blond hair.

"I'll get some drinks," said Balvan. He disappeared into the back and returned with a tray holding three cans of coke and some local snacks. Tally loved the spiciness of the nuts and crisps, and together they tucked in and chatted happily about the differences in their countries.

After a while Balvan looked at his watch. "We need to go, Tally, if you want to have a look around."

"Can I come too?" pleaded Aditi.

"Sorry, little one." Balvan shook his head. "We will walk a long way and very fast."

Aditi stuck out her bottom lip and looked as if she were about to cry.

"Don't be sad, Aditi," Tally soothed. "I'll see you again soon. In fact," she sneaked a look at Balvan, "if it's OK, I'll come tomorrow afternoon and bring you a present." She wasn't sure what, but she would find something.

Aditi's enormous eyes shone with happiness, and she held onto Tally's hand as they went through the shop to say goodbye to Mrs Chabra, busy sewing at her old pedal machine.

CHAPTER TEN

"Oh, it did not happen overnight. The sculptor toiled for many years over the task, working exclusively in my cave. And then only when he could take time from his daily commitments and family life. He would sit, cross-legged, on the floor and fashion each individual feather of my wings. He was meticulous. He refused to reveal the work to me until he finished. I had to exercise patience."

The heat hit Tally as they left the shade of the house, but it was so much more comfortable in her silk clothes that she didn't mind. They joined the surging mass of traffic and pedestrians, inching along the edge of the hot, dusty road.

There was no proper pavement, and they had to squeeze between stationary motorcycles and carts that looked as if they'd been abandoned.

It was scary! There were so many cars, motorbikes, painted lorries, and people. Bicycles wobbled past almost invisible under their cargoes of plastic containers, bags of fodder, tins and boxes.

Balvan pointed to some green and yellow three-wheeler motorbikes with little cabins on them for passengers. "Bet you don't have those in England," he shouted, raising his voice above the din.

Tally shook her head.

"They're called tuk-tuks," he continued. "They're taxis. Much cheaper than the cars."

At that moment, a motorbike carrying a father, mother and TWO children swooped past them. Tally stared, amazed.

"Don't worry," Balvan joked. "The dad's wearing a crash helmet."

A lorry with half a dozen men standing in the open back brushed a bit too close and Tally jumped sideways, bumping into Balvan.

"Are you OK?"

Tally swallowed. "How do you cope with all this traffic? I feel as if I'll get squashed at any moment!" she admitted, as he pulled her into the overhang of a half-finished building with trees growing out of it.

"There is a special way to walk in traffic in India," Balvan explained. "Just walk at a constant pace. Don't stop or change direction. The drivers know you are there and if you keep walking, they will figure out where they need to go."

Tally watched the other pedestrians crossing the street or walking among the cars and caught on. No one hurried, nor did they try to dodge vehicles – and, yes, the traffic flowed around them.

"OK." She nodded. "I'll try."

She followed Balvan across the busy road. A little further along they turned a corner and came to a street market. There were no stalls as Tally was used to; instead, the vendors dumped their produce on the ground and sat in a hole in the centre.

Tally stopped in front of a pile of unusual fruits and vegetables. "What are they?" she asked, pointing to what looked like gigantic pears with prickly skins.

"Ah, we call them quora." Balvan frowned. "I don't know the English word. They are like spaghetti inside. They don't smell nice, but they taste something like mango or pineapple."

Tally resolved to ask Abha when she got home and practised the word quora so she wouldn't forget. She followed her nose to the next pile of produce; it smelled better than the perfume department in a store at home. At first glance Tally thought it was heaps of coloured cloth, but as she looked closer, she realised the piles were fresh flower petals. She breathed in with delight.

An old lady sat in the middle threading the petals onto strands of cotton to make garlands or streamers. But even more fascinating were triangles, big enough to wear as shawls, hanging on a wooden frame behind her. Tally realised they were made of cotton and petals too.

"What are they for?" she asked.

"People wear them at weddings, or they make offerings in temples to their gods," Balvan replied.

"Do you have many gods?"

"Thousands!" He laughed. "We have a god for every single thing in India. Come, I'll show you one." He took Tally's arm and steered her between two stalls of oranges, until they were face to face with a pile of what looked like very British junk.

"Meet Ganesha," Balvan announced, and pointed to a nine-inch statue of a pot-bellied man with an elephant head and four arms.

"He's gorgeous," Tally declared. "What is he god of?"

"He destroys obstacles and brings success." Balvan grinned. "He's incredibly popular!"

"I'll bet," Tally agreed as she looked at the rest of the pile of junk.

"Who's this?" she asked, indicating a painting thrown on the top of the pile. "It looks like St George and the Dragon, except that St George is in Indian costume." The dragon looked ferocious; his teeth were bigger than the St George figure.

"I'm not sure," Balvan admitted. He spoke in Hindi to the stall owner. "OK, he says it's Ahi – sometimes called Vritra – and the deity slaying him is Indra."

"So, is Vit… Vritra a god?"

"Some people refer to him as a god. Actually, he is a demon – what we call Asuras."

Tally rolled the word around on her tongue. Asuras, quora and dhoti – now she knew three Indian words to wow Dad. Maybe she could learn the language and become an interpreter.

They waited as a man, almost bent double under a stack of bamboo, squeezed past, then they skirted round the junk stall to take an alley leading to a smaller street. The noise of the cars faded, and the tarmac became dust. A few sad trees poked out between awnings of dirty tarpaulins supported by poles. There was litter everywhere, but no people. The only movement was some birds hopping in a tree, screeching and squawking. Tally shaded her eyes to see them better.

Balvan approached an entrance almost hidden between carts and piles of logs for firewood. He held back a string curtain for Tally to enter. "This is where I have to get the machine part," he explained.

"Do you mind if I wait here?" she asked. She wanted to watch those birds. Were they parrots?

"Of course not," Balvan agreed. "I won't be a minute." And he brushed past her to go in.

Tally stepped over the empty plastic wrappings and old newspapers strewn in front of the building. She needed a better spot to see the birds. They were so pretty! They had striped wings and crests with peach-coloured bodies. No, they weren't parrots, but she didn't know what they were. She'd have to ask Dad; he was great at identifying birds.

Just then she heard a different screech. She stood on her tiptoes to peer over the carts that lined the street.

There! Halfway down the street was a tall man pulling a little girl out of a car that sped away in the opposite direction. He was unshaven and wearing a grubby shirt with a dhoti. Somehow he looked familiar, but Tally wasn't sure why. The girl was crying and trying to pull away. Tally bit her lip and strained her neck to get a better look. What should she do? If she ran to get Balvan, they might disappear.

The man saw her staring. He grinned and shrugged his shoulders, gesturing to the girl as if to show she was being very naughty. Then, in a loud voice, he said, "You must do as your Bapu says. Now come inside. You can go out to play later." And he pushed open the door to a house and shoved the child inside, before turning to Tally and giving her a friendly wave.

They had gone. But Tally was suspicious. Why would he speak to his child in English? For her benefit? And why did he look familiar? She lifted the pendant to her lips.

"Did you see that, Jophiel?" she whispered. "Do you think he was her dad?"

The pendant moved in her hand.

"*I saw nothing,*" Jophiel replied inside her head. "*The woodpile was in the way. What happened?*"

Tally told him. "They went into that house with the torn awning. Can you take a look?"

"*I cannot separate myself from the pendant, Tally, I am bound to it and to you. If you want to look, we must go together.*"

Tally hesitated. She shouldn't really wander away; and anyway, she was scared. Maybe the man *was* kidnapping the girl. But what could she do about it? She shook her head. She was being melodramatic; he probably was the girl's father, and he'd be annoyed if she interfered. She'd be sensible, stay here, and tell Balvan what she'd seen.

She felt the pendant vibrate. *"Follow your heart, child,"* Jophiel urged. *"If you think there's something wrong, there probably is."*

So much for sense! Tally took a deep breath and started towards the building into which the man and the girl had disappeared. She would listen at a window. And anyway, she wasn't alone – she had Jophiel.

As she got closer she slowed down and edged up to a shuttered window near to the door. She couldn't see anything through the slats, so she put her ear against the wood.

"Can you *hear anything?"* she whispered to Jophiel. She held the pendant near to the window.

"Not inside," he answered, *"but I can hear a child crying under our feet."*

Tally looked down but there was nothing apart from bare earth. "Are they in a cellar?"

"*I don't think so. The sound is moving,*" he murmured. "*Towards the middle of the street.*"

Tally felt the pendant tug gently away from her towards the direction the cries were travelling. Jophiel couldn't go unless she did. She glanced back, hoping Balvan might have emerged, but there was no sign. She should wait.

But that little girl could be in danger!

CHAPTER ELEVEN

"Neither did the stone mason perform his task willingly, but because of a debt to Sarathiel. He begrudged the time spent in my cold dark prison, but we became accustomed to each other. And over the years, through his complaints, sorrows, hardships and joys, I learned a vast amount about the trivial mundanities of man."

As they got further away from where she was supposed to be, Tally hung back.

"Can you still hear anything?" she asked Jophiel.

"It is intermittent, but the child continues to cry. Do you want to go on?"

Tally hesitated. For the sound to have moved this far, the man must be taking the girl along an underground passageway. So maybe her theory about secret tunnels was right. But what could she do?

She could follow and find out where the tunnel led. She looked round. Right now, she couldn't see anyone, but if she carried on walking she would come to a busy street, and then she would stand out with her colouring. People would wonder what an English child was doing wandering around alone. Making another quick decision, she hid her hair under her scarf.

"Let's go," she said, and keeping her head down she hurried along the road. She hated to think how terrified the girl must be if she really had been kidnapped.

"Can't you send her some comfort, Jophiel?" Tally pleaded.

"*She is too far away,*" he responded. "*Maybe I can send a few calming thoughts, but, though it is brutal, we need her to cry so we can follow.*"

They were walking in the opposite direction to the market and the small street ended at a busy road that circled the town. There were more people here and Tally kept her face to the ground. No one challenged her. She was just another child, hurrying home from school or errands. Either that or Jophiel was doing something to hide her, she thought.

The pendant tugged at her to cross the road and she hesitated.

"Are you sure it's a child you can hear, Jophiel, and not just some rats squeaking in the sewers or something?"

The chain on the pendant stiffened as it pulled insistently. "*I can promise you there is nothing wrong with my hearing,*" the angel assured her. "*There were also two sets of footsteps, but I can't hear the child's feet dragging any more.*"

*And they are going faster. I think the man must be carrying
her."*

Tally stared across the road. On the other side was a
small group of pigs snuffling around in a pile of rubbish
on a dusty wasteland. Would they have to cross that? She
was scared to leave the safety of the built-up area. And
what about the man who had been driving the car? Was he
around still?

"Are you sure we have to cross?" Tally asked in a small
voice.

Jophiel's voice came into her mind. *"I am, but do not fear,
Tally. You are not alone. You walk with an angel."*

Swallowing hard, Tally started to cross the road in the
way Balvan had taught her. She reached the edge of the
wasteland and took stock of her bearings. Now she was
able to see that the empty stretch of land dipped away to
an expanse of water. There was a lopsided wooden shed
directly in front of her. A boat shed? Was that where the
man had taken the little girl? Tally ran towards it, half

hoping she was wrong. She didn't want to bump into the kidnapper.

But when they got to the boathouse, Jophiel tugged her around the other side of it to the edge of the lake.

She looked across the water. Right there in the middle stood the old hotel. She had approached it from a different angle this time, but it was definitely the same one.

"*They are going underneath the lake*," Jophiel announced. "*We cannot follow any further.*"

"But at least we know this much," Tally panted. "And it looks like I was right. There *are* secret tunnels. Let's go and tell someone."

She turned back towards the town. In the heat and the haze, the low grey buildings looked like a single wall, and it was impossible to see the alley where they'd come out.

"Jophiel," she panicked, "I'm lost."

Tally felt as if his wings circled her. "*You're not lost, my child*," the angel comforted. "*You are with me, and as I led you here, so I will lead you back. I think we should go to your home. Balvan will have finished his errand and will look for you there. Walk this way."*

Tally walked as quickly as possible. She knew Jophiel would lead her the right way, but she was still terrified for the stolen girl, and so afraid of being seen by one of the kidnappers. And there was another worry nagging at her: Dad's reaction. If Balvan had gone to her house without her, Dad was going to be furious. And how could she explain what she'd done? She could tell them what she'd *seen*, but she'd have to say *she* had heard the girl crying under the ground. And as she couldn't mention Jophiel, how could she convince them she hadn't been in any danger?

This could be bad.

As soon as Tally was in sight of her house she ran, ignoring her exhaustion, thirst, and dusty clothes.

At a shout from the garden, she looked up to see Balvan waving and yelling something in Hindi towards the house.

Raj's voice boomed out in response. She heard him shouting to her dad.

"You go, Aaron. I will tell the police Tally has returned."

Then Dad was shooting out of the front door and running towards her. He grabbed Tally in a hug. Then he pulled her into the hallway, held her out at arm's length and yelled, "Where have you been?"

"I...I can explain," Tally stammered.

Dad's expression hardened. "What do you mean, you can explain?" His voice turned to ice. "Unless somebody forcibly removed you from the spot where Balvan had asked you to wait, which it's clear they didn't, what can there be to explain?" Tally stood, head down and burning with embarrassment that Balvan should see this. Dad was relentless. He told her how selfish, thoughtless, uncaring, and inconsiderate she'd been, and grounded her for two weeks.

"I saw a little girl being kidnapped," she whispered when Dad stopped to take a breath. "And I tried to see where she was being taken."

"You saw what?" Raj demanded, his mobile phone pressed to his ear. "What made you think the child was being kidnapped?"

"A man dragged her into a house and when I went to listen at the window I heard cries underground, so I followed."

"What do you mean, you followed?" Dad demanded.

"I followed the sound of her crying. They went all the way to that lake with the hotel." Tally knew it sounded lame. No one was going to believe her.

"Why didn't you call me?" Balvan growled.

There was nothing anyone could say to make Tally feel any worse. She wished Jophiel would appear now and help her out. What good was an angel that only she saw and heard?

Raj's calm voice took charge. "The police are on their way. You can tell them what you think you saw, and they will take it from there."

As the words left his lips, the doorbell rang. Abha, who had remained silent, her face like a stone, let in two police officers, a sergeant and a constable.

The sergeant looked kindly at Tally. "We are very relieved you have returned, young miss. You must be careful about wandering around alone in an unfamiliar city. There are always dangers."

"I know," Tally replied, in awe of the turbaned police officer. "I heard about the missing children. But I saw a girl being taken today."

The two officers' eyebrows shot up.

"Are you sure?" asked the constable. "Did you see where she was taken?"

"I can show you the house," Tally faltered.

"Let's go." The sergeant snapped into action and took her, Dad and Balvan to his car, while Raj followed behind.

They needed Balvan to direct them to the right street; Raj would bring them home afterwards. Abha stayed behind, but she gave Tally's shoulder a quick squeeze on her way out.

Tally's heart was thumping as she pointed out the house, and the constable knocked on the door.

Nothing. Tally was desperate for the police to search further.

"I didn't see anyone leave," she persisted. "Do you think there's a secret way out? Like a tunnel or something?"

The two officers grinned.

"What a lively imagination!" the sergeant said. "Clearly you like to read mystery books." He started back to his car. "We will find out who owns the house and ask to see inside. It's a police matter now. I suggest you go home."

Tally was relieved as she, Dad and Balvan piled into Raj's car. She hadn't wanted that man to see her again. She had done what she could.

"Balvan, we'll drop you off at home," said Dad, whose lips were a grim straight line.

"Thank you, Uncle," Balvan muttered. Tally sneaked a sideways look at him. He was sitting as far away from her as possible on the back seat of the car, and staring out of the window so he didn't have to talk to her. Tears pricked her eyes. She'd been so excited to have made a friend already, but Balvan probably never wanted to see her again.

Before long they were outside Balvan's house and his mum came running out, smiling a welcome. As Balvan got out of the car and shut the door, his mum fired questions at him, her smile fading. Soon she was yelling. Mr Chabra charged out of the house and shouted more questions. Balvan was looking horrified, and Raj was throwing open the car door to join in. Dad and Tally followed.

Raj translated. "Aditi has gone missing. She told her mother that she was going with you and Balvan. She must have followed on her own."

Tally felt her tummy drop. Please don't let it be true! Aditi would be somewhere nearby; or on her way back, once she had failed to catch up with her brother. But Tally knew in her heart that too many hours had passed. Aditi would have come home by now if she'd been able.

"This is all my fault," Tally whispered.

Dad heard her and took her hand. "Actually, this isn't your fault," he said briskly. "Aditi decided to follow you before you went AWOL." The glimmer of relief she felt disappeared at his next words. "However, we might have found out sooner if you hadn't done what you did."

Raj approached and Dad asked him what they could do to help.

"Nothing, my friend." The Indian doctor shook his head. "I will take you home. Balvan and his parents will rouse the neighbourhood to help look for Aditi." Already people were shouting and running in and out of the houses along the street. Mrs Chabra sat in a corner of the shop, rocking backwards and forwards and wailing.

"No need to take us," said Dad. "We're only round the corner. We'll walk." He went to speak to Balvan, who was making frantic calls to all his school friends on his mobile, and Tally followed him. She couldn't leave without saying *something* to her friend.

"Please let me know if there's anything I can do," Dad was saying. "Tell us when you find Aditi, won't you?"

The boy nodded but didn't speak. His grief showed in his handsome face, and Tally wished she could comfort him.

"I'm so, so sorry," she whispered, "Please…" Her voice trailed away. What could she say?

Balvan gave a curt nod and turned away.

CHAPTER TWELVE

"This was God's Almighty Plan?"

Aditi didn't come home that day. Or that night. Or even the following day. Three days later, she was still missing, and it was as if the entire street had gone into mourning.

Tally tried to concentrate on her online schoolwork, but it was almost impossible. Most of the time she stared out of the window, wishing she could join in the search. Balvan and his friends had passed the gate many times looking for who knew what, but he didn't even glance at Tally's window, never mind knock on the door.

Tally knew Balvan blamed her for Aditi's disappearance, and in a way he was right. She felt wretched and helpless. Abha tried to occupy her by giving her odd jobs to do, but Tally couldn't concentrate on those either. Her only comfort was Jophiel, and her only outlet for her frustration her pin.

"Nobody's telling me anything," Tally complained to the angel when they were alone in her room. "Dad's had loads of phone calls, but he won't tell me what people are saying, just that there's no news. It makes me so mad!"

Jophiel was sitting on the windowsill, his face in shadow, his wings edged in sunlight. "You did your best, child. You must hope that your information was valuable."

"I wish *you* could go and look," mourned Tally, not for the first time. "I know you can't leave the pendant, but even if you just appeared to others, things would be much easier. Then I could prove what we saw and heard the other day."

She thought Jophiel looked uncomfortable. Could an angel feel uncomfortable? And although she was used to the fact that she never saw his face clearly, she knew he had turned away. Suspicion crept into her head.

"*Can* you appear to other people?" she probed.

The angel hesitated. "I would be in significant danger if I did, child. For thousands of years I have hidden in the pendant. I must stay hidden, except to the bearer."

"But why?" she demanded.

"Dangerous forces are everywhere. Demons, fallen angels - they search for me. I can tell you only that." And she knew the subject was closed.

At that moment Tally heard a knock at the front door and she rushed out of her room in time to see Raj enter and shake her Dad's hand.

For once, Dad didn't send her away.

"I'm afraid they found nothing," Raj said in Tally's direction. "They spoke to the man who had the house, though not till the next day, and he confirmed that he had been reprimanding his daughter and remembers seeing you. He was very cooperative and allowed them to search the house and backyard. There were no secret doors or passageways."

Tally felt herself going red. "What about the lake hotel?" she ventured.

"They have searched it many times. There are no dungeons full of stolen children, no hidden doors or tunnels under the ground. The only mystery is why the lake doesn't dry up, and that is a geological question, not a criminal one. The sergeant was correct, you have a vivacious imagination."

Tally flushed and bit back a retort. She knew she was right about the tunnel; she just couldn't prove it.

Mumbling an excuse, she went back to her room. She needed to think and plan. She needed to talk to Jophiel.

"If only I could speak to Balvan," she grumbled, as she paced around her small bedroom. Jophiel had returned to his seat at the window, the sunlight shimmering across his wings. "Can't you do *anything*?" she pleaded.

The angel put his palms together. "If Balvan were close enough, I might make him believe he needs to seek you out on your own. But I can't do it from a distance."

"Why didn't you do that before?" Tally cried. "Why didn't you make everyone believe me when the police were here?"

Jophiel sighed. "I have been on earth too long, Tally. Unlike my brothers, who have the power to convince a prison full of guards that they see nothing, I can only guide the thoughts of one person at a time. There were too many people that day."

Tally exhaled. "OK. We need to think of a way to get near to Balvan. What if we wait in the garden? He'll go past some time. Could you sort of catch him?"

"You might wait a very long time," Jophiel mused.

"I know. It's not much of a plan," she conceded. She slumped on to the bed. Then she brightened. "Wait though! Can you get Dad to believe we should visit Balvan's family? Then, when we're close to him, I'll slip him a note. I'll ask him to meet me, and you can influence him – or whatever you want to call it. Make him want to do it."

"You are suggesting a lot of interfering with human thought." Jophiel shook his wing feathers, making the reflected sunlight dance. "But it is possible."

"Well, what are we waiting for?" Tally cried.

"Let us wait till Raj departs, shall we?" came the dry answer. Tally rolled her eyes.

They got their opportunity over lunch.

"We should call on Balvan's family this afternoon," said Dad, with a faraway expression in his eyes. "Show our support and ask if there's anything they need."

Tally nodded her head, her mouth too full of chickpea curry and rice to speak. The pendant glowed against her chest.

"Perhaps we'll go later on, when Balvan will be back from school," Dad amended, and Tally silently applauded her angel.

CHAPTER THIRTEEN

"The sculptor was an old man at the completion of the task. He spent the last years forming the unbreakable chain. He carved each minute link from the stone, and yet it resembled the finest metal. Sarathiel joined us for the great unveiling and to witness my transition."

Balvan was at home when Tally and her Dad arrived, hot and dusty despite it being a short walk.

Mr Chabra greeted them and they entered the cool shop. Balvan stood nearby, but not near enough for Tally to slip him her note. However, she felt the pendant glow, and instantly he glanced at her. He approached and asked how she was.

This was her chance. Taking his hand, as a friend would, she asked, "How are *you*, more to the point?" while pressing the tightly folded paper into his palm. His eyes widened slightly.

"It's awful," he croaked, visibly struggling. "My mother hasn't worked since A… Aditi was taken." He turned away and Tally ached for his pain. He brushed his hand across his eyes. "I will bring you a drink," he muttered, and went into the back of the house.

When he returned with four glasses on a tray, he looked directly at Tally and gave her a slight nod. Excellent, she thought, he's read the note and agreed. She nodded back and, with her back to the adults, made a thumbs-up sign.

Balvan handed the drinks around and they stood drinking in an uncomfortable silence. After a few minutes

Dad asked once more if he could do anything, and when Mr Chabra said no, he and Tally went home.

It was tough waiting till midnight, the time Tally had asked Balvan to meet her in the garden. They needed to be alone for what she planned.

The hours dragged. Tally left the shutters on her balcony door unlatched, even though she had been warned *not* to; shutters were for security, not only for shade. But she didn't want the noise of the bolts waking her Dad when she crept out. Fortunately the house was single storey, so to get to the garden she could climb over the railing surrounding her balcony.

Tally set the alarm on her mobile and put it under her pillow to muffle the sound, but there was no way she was going to sleep. She was far too nervous and excited, and she kept going over the plan she had agreed with Jophiel. He had been less enthusiastic than Tally had hoped.

"But why not?" she'd begged repeatedly.

"It would be, what is that phrase you humans use so much these days? Unethical."

Tally had looked at him sideways. "Haven't you ever done anything you shouldn't?"

His light had dimmed, and he'd fallen silent. Then he'd sighed. "My role is to guide you to do the right thing, Tally. Not join you in your tricks. However," Tally had held her breath, "I feel you are on to something here, so, just this one time, I will collaborate."

At last, it was midnight. For ease and camouflage Tally pulled on black jeans and a dark T-shirt. Then she slipped out onto the balcony.

Glad of the streetlights, she hurried to the perimeter of the garden. The bush where she had first seen Balvan was where she had suggested they meet. Her heart was thudding, and her mouth was dry. Then she remembered Jophiel was with her, and everything was all right. She was invincible, and as brave as a she-wolf. Even when

Balvan hissed her name from under the branches of a bougainvillea bush, she didn't jump.

She was so pleased to see him, she threw her arms around him. To her delight, he returned the hug with equal warmth before they sat down on the dusty ground to talk. Tally started by repeating her story about the kidnapping and her trek following the underground cries.

Balvan didn't look at her. "I know all this already, Tally," he said. "I thought you had something new to tell me."

"Well, for one thing - I remembered why the man looked familiar. He was one of the ones I saw at the Taj Mahal."

"And that helps how, exactly?" Balvan said dryly.

Tally took a deep breath. It was time to put her plan into action. She braced herself to lie convincingly. "There's something you need to know about me," she announced. "I have certain psychic powers. I swear to you I know that little girl was taken along underground passages."

Balvan's eyebrows shot up. "Psychic powers? Really? Prove it!"

"I will." She sat up straight. "Think of a colour."

He looked startled. "I'm thinking of one."

The pendant grew warm on her chest.

"*Indigo,*" revealed Jophiel inside her head.

"Indigo!" Tally repeated, in a low but triumphant voice.

Balvan looked astonished, but insisted, "That was just coincidence."

"Well, I can see you might think that. So, try a number instead. Not a low one, something in the thousands."

He blinked. "I'm ready."

"*Four thousand five hundred and ninety-one.*"

She said the number, and Balvan's mouth dropped open. "Do another one," he urged.

"Six thousand one hundred and twenty," she repeated after Jophiel's prompt.

Balvan stared at her. "How do you do that?"

"I told you, I have some very limited sort of psychic powers. I can't really explain it to you, but I *could* hear that little girl being dragged under the ground. Somehow, the man tricked the police. We MUST investigate, Balvan, you and me. Because I believe that wherever they took that girl, Aditi will be in the same place."

"Why haven't you told your dad all this?" Balvan demanded. "Surely he knows about your special powers?"

"It's complicated," Tally insisted. "I shouldn't really tell you. But I want to find Aditi. Why don't we go now?"

"Are you crazy? I don't want my parents to think I've gone missing as well."

"But surely there's no time to lose if we're to find your sister?"

Pain etched his face. "It's too dangerous at night. And we need to be able to see. We will go in the daylight."

"But I'm grounded," Tally protested. "Dad won't let me go off somewhere with you. Not after last time."

Balvan pursed his lips. Tally, disappointed he didn't like her plan, itched to plead with him, but she kept quiet.

"I'll think of something," Balvan said eventually. "I'll come tomorrow morning. Be ready. And wear Indian clothes so you blend in."

CHAPTER FOURTEEN

"The stone mason revealed the effigy, full of pride for his years of toil. I was aghast.

'But I don't look like that.' I protested.

Sarathiel smiled. 'You do to the sculptor,' he said gently. 'And to each person who beholds you, you will appear differently. In this way, you will remain hidden.'"

Next morning Tally hoped Balvan had come up with a good plan to make Dad allow her out. She dressed in her salwar kemees anyway. With her blond hair tied back into a ponytail, and the matching scarf draped over her head and hiding her face, no one would know, from a distance, that she wasn't another local girl out with her brother. About to pull on strappy sandals, she hesitated. Perhaps not the best choice if they had a lengthy walk; or had to run. She pushed the shoes back into the cupboard and pulled on trainers instead. Abha often wore practical-looking Nikes under her salwar kemees, so Tally didn't think it would attract any attention.

To her relief, Dad agreed that she could visit Mrs Chabra.

"I'll be at the hospital all day, so it'll give you something to do," Dad said. "But stay with Balvan this time, Natalie!"

Tally promised, and she and Balvan set off. They were halfway down the road when Tally realised she'd forgotten her mobile. She shrugged. Too late to go back.

"We'll watch from a safe distance to begin with," Balvan reminded her. "If there's no movement, we'll knock. If someone answers, I'll say I am collecting signatures for a petition." He pulled a large note pad out of his shoulder satchel. It had several names scrawled on it.

"How did you get those?"

"From a project we did at school last year," Balvan said. "But no one will know that."

This time they didn't stop to enjoy the busy market. They walked quickly, and were soon turning into the quiet street where Tally had seen the little girl being kidnapped. The heat was already stifling, and Tally sighed with relief when they stopped in the shade of the trees where she'd seen the birds and hid behind some empty packing cases. They had a good view of the house into which the man and girl had disappeared.

Balvan nudged her. "Is that him?"

Tally turned to see Balvan pointing to a man exiting the next building, before jumping into a car and driving away.

"That's him!" Tally gasped. "But that's not the right door." She pointed at the adjoining house. "That's where I sent the police."

Balvan narrowed his eyes. "So, the police searched the wrong house. The tunnel, if it exists, must be in the house he just left. Come on." They left their hiding place and approached the door.

"Stay behind me," murmured Balvan as he knocked. They waited. Nothing happened, and he knocked again. No one came, so he tried the handle.

"It's locked."

"That doesn't surprise me," Tally replied and turned away. "Let's try the other house."

"Why?"

"I've had an idea. Go on, knock," she insisted. He did. Again, no answer.

"Try the handle," Tally whispered.

Balvan turned the handle, and the door opened without resistance. They held their breath, waiting for someone to shout, but nothing happened. They slipped inside and shut the door.

They were in a room containing a sofa and some mats. Through an opening they could see another with two beds. An archway led to a small kitchen with a dirt floor. Through the open back door they could see a small yard. Tally's heart thumped as they sprinted across the first room, into the kitchen and out into the yard. She was convinced there'd be a door or a gate linking this house to the one next door.

Nothing. Only a square patch of dirt surrounded by a rickety bamboo fence. Most remarkable was the lack of rubbish. Litter always collected in corners and along fences. No one ever cleared it away. But here was just dusty ground that looked as if someone had swept it with a hard brush.

Tally swallowed her disappointment. She'd been positive the two houses were linked.

"We'd better go," Balvan whispered.

Tally followed him back across the yard. But before she reached the kitchen door, she felt the pendant glow warmly. She allowed Jophiel into her mind. *"Look at the fence, Tally. I detect something strange in that corner."*

Tally broke away from Balvan and hurried to the corner of the yard where the fence met the building. That was weird. She could hear water. She looked for a source but didn't find one.

"The fence is not normal," Jophiel persisted. *"There is power around it."*

Tally stared at the bamboo, which seemed pretty ordinary. Then, cautiously, she stretched out her hand to touch it. But instead of encountering rough bark, her fingers slid into icy water. If that wasn't strange enough, the water and the fence disappeared, leaving a gap large enough for two people to pass through. Gasping, she pulled her hand back and the bamboo fence, or the illusion of it, reappeared.

"What the...?"

Balvan rushed up behind her. "Come *on*, Tally. I thought you were following me. Are you OK? What are you staring at?"

"Watch this," she said. She stretched her hand towards the fence again. As the gap reappeared, they were able to see an identical yard on the other side. Balvan cried out in alarm and pulled Tally away. Instantly the bamboo was back in place.

"That's not possible," Balvan muttered. "What sort of black magic is this?" He stretched out a shaking hand to touch the fence, snatching it back as if it had stung him. "It's just solid bamboo." He glared at her. "What did you do?"

"I didn't do anything except touch it," Tally insisted. And to prove it, she reached out again. Once more, she felt water before the fence disappeared.

They stared at each other.

"Let's get out of here," Balvan croaked. "We can go to the police and show this to them. They will have to act now."

But Tally didn't feel scared. Maybe because she was used to strange things happening since an angel had come into her life.

"Let's have a quick peek," she pleaded. "Then we'll go." She touched the bamboo again and marvelled as it disappeared once more. "Look! There's no one there – the yard is empty. And we know the house is empty because we rang the doorbell."

Tally stepped through the gap and the way behind her closed, leaving Balvan on the other side.

Suddenly, the pendant burned on her chest, and Jophiel's form blazed beside her. Instantly Tally was filled with a wave of terror that nearly knocked her off her feet.

At the same time she heard Balvan's panicked cry. "Come back, Tally. It doesn't work for me. All I can feel is the wood."

Jophiel put his hands on her shoulders. "You must go back," he cried. "There is great danger here. This power is evil."

Before she could react, Balvan's voice hissed through the fence. "Quick, open the gap, someone just came into the house. Let me through."

Tally thrust her hand against the fence, her heart pounding. Jophiel disappeared as Balvan rushed to her side and pulled on her arm.

"Hurry. We need to hide."

But there was nowhere in the yard. It was identical to the one they had just left, including no litter.

Their only hope was the house. They raced through the open back door, then slowed to give their eyes time to adjust to the dimness after the sunshine. What should have been the kitchen was empty – no furniture, no cupboards, no sink or utensils anywhere. An empty space.

On the far side was a door. As in the other house, it led to two rooms. They knew the street door was locked, but they could wait. Hopefully whoever was in the other house would leave soon, and they could go back the way they'd come.

But they hesitated too long. Before they could cross the room, a trapdoor opened in the floor in front of them and two men clambered out of the opening, carrying sticks and whips.

The men yelled in surprise then, in two strides, were beside them. One of them grabbed Balvan's arms while the other snatched Tally round the waist, picking her up with one sweep.

Tally was too shocked even to shout. She had been kidnapped!

CHAPTER FIFTEEN

"Sarathiel praised the stonemason. 'It is a masterpiece. Even without the spirit of Jophiel, you could provide for generations of your family from the proceeds of such a piece. But you know it is not yours to sell nor keep. For Jophiel to return to the world, you must gift the pendant freely. And henceforth, to preserve the secret, it must always be gifted freely.'"

Tally drew in a breath to scream. But as she did, the man's hand clamped over her mouth. It almost suffocated her; his skin was coarse and dry, and she smelled sweat, dirt and stale curry on his fingers. She saw Balvan fighting and kicking hard, but his captor had him in a headlock and anyway, the two men were huge. Tally and Balvan didn't stand a chance.

Mentally she screamed, "*Jophiel, hear me*" and he filled her head, as the men dragged her and Balvan through the trapdoor. "*Save us!*"

"*You know I cannot do anything physically, Tally,*" the angel cried. "*But I am here with you.*"

Great. A helpless guardian angel. "*Can't you make them let us go?*" She fought and wriggled. She did *not* want to be dragged down those stairs.

"*I can't influence two people at once,*" Jophiel snapped. "*I am sorry, Tally. This is all horrifying. But I can calm you, so you can think.*" And the fight went out of her as the angel's wings embraced her.

The man grunted in surprise and almost dropped her. That alone would have been a result, but he shifted her weight and continued his descent. Tally heard Balvan grunting and struggling. Then came the sound of a fist connecting with flesh, and there was silence except for the slap of the men's feet on the stone and their heavy breathing.

"Jophiel," Tally cried in her head. *"Is Balvan OK?"*

"He has been knocked out. He is unconscious, but he will recover. You are entering a cave."

Tally felt the air change as the walls opened out. Her attacker took a dozen more strides, then flung her to the floor. She yelled as the stone connected with her body, and she grabbed at her headscarf as it slipped off her head. They threw Balvan down next to her, flinging his satchel far away. Tally caught the unconscious boy before his head hit the wall. She stared around the dungeon, which was lit by burning sconces placed at intervals on the walls.

One man spoke in English. "Well, well! What do we have here?"

Tally flinched and glared as he thrust out his hand to grab her blond ponytail and hold it up to show his colleague.

"Exquisite," he breathed. Tally jerked her head to pull her hair free. The men laughed and said something in their own language. That infuriated her even more. She couldn't crawl away from them because she was holding on to Balvan.

"Let us go," she shouted. "People know where we are. They'll come looking for us. You can't get away with this. My father will be here any minute, and he'll bring the police."

"And they will find nothing," the man jeered. "The question is, how did you get through the water? How did you find it? Ranbir will be very angry. He'll want to know how you defeated the magic."

His eyes lighted on her pendant and Tally went cold as he dropped her ponytail and grasped the angel effigy. *No, please no. Not my angel. Why didn't I hide it away? Jophiel!*

The man examined the statue, turning it over in his hand. "You won't be needing this where you're going," he smirked, and with a hard flick of his wrist, yanked the chain to snap it.

Tally flinched, anticipating pain as the chain should have cut into her flesh. But it didn't hurt at all. Neither did it break. He pulled again, and she cried out, more in anger, but it occurred to her she should probably pretend it hurt. "Ow! Stop!"

Again, the chain didn't break. "Take it off!" he ordered, stepping back, and gesturing at her with his stick. With fingers trembling and fumbling, Tally turned the chain round and round to find the tiny clasp.

It had gone. There was no clasp – no way to open the chain.

"I can't. It doesn't undo."

Once again he stooped to her level and ran the chain round in his meaty, smelly hand. He twisted and pulled, grumbled and muttered, but in the end had to give up.

"No matter." He shrugged. "I will bring the cutter." And turning to his colleague, he fired off rapid instructions in Hindi as they moved to the other side of the cavern.

At that moment, Balvan stirred. Tally helped him sit up and lean against the wall.

"How do you feel?" she whispered.

He groaned and clutched his head. "I have a colossal headache. Where are we?"

"They've dragged us down some steps to this cave. We haven't gone far. We must be still under the house. I haven't found out much, I can't understand what they say unless they speak to me in English." Tally kept her voice low, talking close to Balvan's ear so she didn't alert the men. They seemed to be arguing over the contents of Balvan's satchel. One of them pocketed Balvan's mobile and Tally lost hope.

Balvan cocked his head to listen. He looked anxious.

"What?" Tally nudged him. "What are they saying? What are they going to do to us?"

Balvan whispered back. "They are talking about someone called Ranbir. They say that they don't need to take you to him; that there are enough children and... ah." He hesitated.

"What? What?" Tally urged.

He looked at the floor. "Nothing. It doesn't matter." He shook his head as if he were trying to dislodge a fly. "They will wait for someone called Sanjay to come back. Maybe he is the man you saw." His eyes searched the cavern. "We have to find a way out."

Tally's eyes had had longer to adjust and now she noticed, underneath each fire sconce, a metal ring sunk into the wall. Then she spied an opening at the opposite end to the stairs. That must be the tunnel to the hotel, she thought. She grabbed Balvan's hand and nodded towards the gap. Then, placing her mouth against his ear, she whispered, "We could run down there. It must be the tunnel that we, I mean, I was following the other day."

He whispered back, "Don't you think that's where they intend to take us anyway? We would run into the mouth of the tiger."

Tally knew he was right. But how else were they going to solve this mystery and find Aditi? And it may lead to other tunnels; ways of escape.

She didn't have time to say all this to Balvan, because the men came back and tied their hands and feet, making running anywhere an impossibility.

"You will stay here," said the man who had captured Tally. "When we come back, we will take you," he nodded at Balvan, "to Ranbir and the shrine. As for you," he picked up Tally's hair and rubbed it between his fingers, "we have other plans for you." Then he glanced at her pendant. "And I'll be taking that too," he hissed.

Tally felt as if ants were crawling up and down her spine. She loathed this man touching her. She spat at him, but he just laughed. "Oh, they'll like a bit of spirit," he mocked. He pulled her far enough away from Balvan that they couldn't undo each other's bindings and attached their ropes to separate rings.

It was all over in minutes. The men strode towards the stairs and disappeared through the trapdoor without another word.

The prisoners looked at each other in despair. Now what?

CHAPTER SIXTEEN

"He had had a hard life, this old man who had begun his task as a youth. He was to receive no monetary reward, no accolade for its beauty, no recognition except gratitude."

Tally and Balvan struggled for ages, trying to get out of the ropes. But that only made the knots tighter and rubbed their ankles and wrists raw. Exhausted, Tally gave up and sank back against the wall to rest. She was so thirsty. The dungeon was only the size of a large room, and the smoke from the fire sconces made the atmosphere dense and uncomfortable. She felt sick.

Dad was going to be FURIOUS. He would definitely send her back to England and boarding school now. If they ever got out of this. Tears pricked her eyes. What if she never saw her dad again? And what were those stinking men planning for her? Why didn't they want to take her with Balvan?

She glanced over to him. He had stopped struggling too and was panting.

Balvan wasn't close enough to see the tears running down her cheeks, but Tally turned her head away, just in case. He would be feeling terrible, and she didn't want to make things worse. Anyway, she wanted to talk to Jophiel, and even though she could do that inside her head, she needed space.

"Jophiel, hear me!"

"*I am here, Tally,*" he replied at once. Tally told herself that nothing terrible would happen to them. Jophiel would save them.

"*What's happening? I couldn't understand them, and Balvan isn't telling me everything, that's for sure.*"

"*They spoke about Ranbir, who must be the person in charge. Also about a shrine – I presume, where all the children are being held.*"

"*You tried to stop me,*" she mourned. "*You said the power was evil. Do you think it comes from the shrine?*"

"*I do not know yet.*" Jophiel paused before he spoke again. "*We could face a great peril, Tally. Not just these wicked men, but a power far greater.*" Tally shivered as he continued. "*But you are here now. The only way is forward. We must allow them to take you to Ranbir. Then we can devise a plan to free you and all the children.*"

"*But they said they had different plans for me,*" she argued. "*Do you know what they are?*"

Jophiel spoke firmly. *"Do not be afraid. I will not let them separate you. I will prevent that, at least."*

He hadn't answered her question. Why wouldn't anyone tell her what they planned? Was it so terrible? Were they going to kill her? Tally remembered things she'd read on the internet about people being sacrificed on shrines. Maybe that's what they meant? She shuddered.

"I will protect you to the absolute limits of my power," the angel whispered.

But Tally shut her mind to him. How would he protect her if he couldn't do anything practical? It was all very well sending warm loving feelings, but what she needed now was an avenging angel, wielding a gigantic sword or something; an angel who appeared to others as a monster to frighten them away. Or one who could, at least, undo these ropes cutting into her skin. She wriggled, then wished she hadn't as the pain in her wrists and ankles burned with a white heat.

"It's better if you keep still," muttered Balvan. "I don't know how we will escape this, Tally. I'm so sorry. Why didn't I tell someone where we were going, so that if we didn't go back they would come and look for us?"

"It wouldn't have made any difference. If they came looking for us, they would have only seen an empty house."

"How did you see the magic in the fence?" Balvan lowered his voice to a whisper. "Is it something to do with your special power? Can you get us out of this?"

Tally pulled a face and was glad he couldn't see it. She presumed it was something to do with Jophiel that allowed her to see the magic, but she couldn't tell that to Balvan. She steered his curiosity in a different direction. "I don't know, but we have to let them take us to where they are holding all the children. That's what we were looking for, isn't it? A way to find Aditi?"

"You're very brave," he murmured.

"Well, they didn't knock me unconscious."

A noise from the stairway interrupted them and three men descended. They must have been confident that no one could see or hear them, as they were making no effort to be stealthy. The leader was the man Tally had seen in the street. He must be Sanjay. Was it only a few days ago? She felt like she'd been in this poxy cavern for ever.

Sanjay stood over her. "So, you thought you would set the police on me, did you? Wait till Ranbir sees you!"

One of the other men spoke in Hindi. Then Tally felt her pendant warm, and Sanjay frowned. His eyes took on the glazed look that Dad's had that one time when Jophiel was influencing his thoughts. "No," Sanjay continued slowly, in English, "we will take her with the boy to Ranbir. If the master ever learned we had sold her, he would punish us very severely."

The men muttered but said no more. Sanjay gestured that they should undo the ropes around the captives' ankles. Tally's original captor did hers and as he approached, he opened his sleeve to show he had a pair of wire clippers hidden.

Tally's breath caught in her throat. She'd forgotten his threat to steal the pendant.

He knelt in front of her and undid the ropes around her ankles. Frozen with fear, she watched him slide the wire cutters out from his sleeve. The greedy anticipation on his face turned to incredulity.

"Where is the necklace?" he hissed. "What have you done with it?"

She looked down, startled. It was staring him in the face. She was about to tell him when she realized that Jophiel must be making him believe that the pendant had disappeared. *Oh, thank you, Jophiel,* she offered silently.

Out loud she said, "You must have broken it without realising it. It fell off after you'd gone, and I kicked it away. Over there." She nodded towards the mouth of the tunnel.

The man snarled, "I will search for it when I come back," and he dragged her to her feet, leaving her to find her balance while he joined his cronies.

Tally's weight buckled as the blood flowed back into her feet, setting them ablaze with pins and needles. She stumbled, and Balvan reached out his tied arms to prop her up.

The men ignored them while they donned head torches and sorted through sacks which they then flung over their shoulders. Then they flicked on the torches, and the first one set off towards the mouth of the tunnel. Sanjay waved his stick for Balvan to follow. The second man went next, and finally Sanjay pushed Tally in, following behind her.

This was it, then. They were going to the old hotel. They would solve the mystery of the stolen children. But what good would solving it do if they couldn't escape?

CHAPTER SEVENTEEN

"The sculptor lowered his head, agreeing to the sacrifice. And my being flowed into the stone, filling it with an ethereal life. The old man gifted the pendant to an ambitious youth in his village, and my journey began."

Tally was conscious of more than Sanjay's presence; despite having blocked him out of her head, Jophiel walked invisibly beside her. It almost felt like he was carrying her, and the long march down the tunnel wasn't as difficult as it might have been – or as it must be for

Balvan, she thought, as she watched him limping on sore feet.

To take her mind off Balvan's pain, and to help ignore the rising temperature in the tunnel, Tally tried to match the way they were going with the way she and Jophiel had gone above ground. But it was impossible. She couldn't gauge how far they had walked that day, or remember each twist and turn as they'd followed the sound of the girl's crying. She relented and allowed Jophiel back inside her head.

"Jophiel, hear me! Can you tell where we are?"

"We are approaching the edge of the lake."

Tally thought back to their pursuit. When she and Jophiel had stopped, their path had ended on the lake's left-hand bank; the hotel had been to their right. So when the tunnel turned left, in the opposite direction from the hotel, Tally questioned Jophiel in surprise.

"Where are we going?" she called out loud, forgetting to keep it a thought.

It didn't matter – Sanjay presumed she was asking him. "I told you," he snarled. "We are going to the shrine."

"Aren't we going to the old hotel?"

"What old hotel? What are you talking about, girl? Stop talking, anyway. Just walk!" And he threatened her with his stick, prompting her to trot a few steps to keep out of its way.

Tally was so, so thirsty... then she wasn't, as Jophiel sent her the sensation of drinking cool water from a frozen glass. How she wished the angel could help Balvan who must be suffering, especially with that headache. But he was too far in front to reach.

Tally could feel the sweat dribbling down her back and her face. Wasn't it supposed to get colder the further you went underground? This tunnel was getting hotter.

At last she could make out other noises apart from the scrunch of their feet. One of them was the sound of running water. Maybe there was an underground river. And there was a loud ominous hissing.

Tally realised the tunnel had ended abruptly. Balvan and the other two men had stopped in its entrance. She stumbled to catch up with them and immediately recoiled: the most terrible stench of garbage hit her nostrils. Sanjay forced her forwards till she was standing next to Balvan in the mouth of the tunnel. It opened onto a cavern so huge Tally could barely see the far side. It must have been as big as a football stadium, but there was no floor. The path they were standing on was only four feet wide; its edge fell away in a sheer drop. It was like standing on the rim of an underground volcano.

Tally stared around, her eyes stinging from smoke and steam rising from the hole. A steady glow of red light showed her the path clinging to the walls of the cavern and circling the pit.

Sanjay dragged them to the edge. "That is where you will be going," he gloated.

Tally teetered and gasped as she looked to where Sanjay was pointing. The sheer rock walls went down, down,

down. Flames leaped up from the bottomless depths and a scorching wind roared into her face. It was a pit of fire! Deep inside the earth! That explained why it was so hot and where the light was coming from. More sweat poured off her forehead and stung her eyes.

The centre of the cavern wasn't empty though; twenty feet below Tally rose a vast column of rugged stone. The top of it looked like an island, cut off on all sides with sheer rock walls falling to the flames. It was rectangular and about the size of a football pitch.

The flattened top of the column seethed with movement. At first Tally thought the whole structure was unstable, but then she realised it wasn't the ground that was moving – it was what was on it: crowds of children and mountains of rotting garbage; plastic bottles, cans, paper, bundles of rags, car tyres, and every so often a great glooping ooze of liquid that defied identification.

Rubbish poured directly onto the children from a giant rocky chute jutting out of the cavern wall high above the island. The sides of the chute were jagged and tall to keep in the contents that oozed down and spewed off the end, which hung about twenty feet above the surface of the platform. The hideous waterfall became a river that flowed stickily across the island, washing up litter on either side, before vanishing into the pit of flames.

Horrified, Tally and Balvan gazed down, their throats closing as they breathed in the stench.

"It's like every bit of rubbish in the world," Tally whispered to Balvan, who nodded, his face pinched with horror.

"What are they doing?" Balvan croaked.

Tally was able to see that the children nearest the centre were frantically scooping the stinking garbage out of the slowly flowing stream. They flung it to the children behind them, who gathered huge armfuls. They then staggered to the long sides of the platform and heaved the garbage into the fires. Clean water fell off the far end of the island and disappeared through a channel in the rock.

Sanjay peered over with them. "They are cleaning the rubbish out of the river," he gloated. "They must make the water pure again before it pours over the edge."

The activity was constant and frenzied. If the children stopped, they would get swept to their deaths by a tsunami of litter.

What made it even more horrifying was that the children weren't making any noise at all. They worked in complete silence, tears running down their cheeks and their faces etched with pain. It stabbed Tally's heart. She gripped Balvan's hand, despite the sweat that made her skin slippery.

Tally turned to Sanjay who was grinning. "So," he laughed, "that is where you will spend the rest of your days. Though it's a shame," he flicked her hair with the tip of his stick. "You will soon be as dirty as the rest of those children, and no one will know what treasure lies underneath the stink. You will never escape, and no one will ever find you."

Tally forced herself to speak through her aching throat. "I don't see any way down. How do we get there?"

Sanjay pointed to the chute with his stick. "Down there, my pretty. Along with the garbage. That's the only way in. There is no way out unless you can fly."

Balvan found his voice at last and, breaking away from Tally's hold, he raged, "But what is it all for? Why are you doing this? Is my sister there?" He craned over the gap and cupped his mouth with his hands. "Aditi!" he yelled, but his voice came back to him on the smoke. None of the children looked up or even indicated that they had heard.

Sanjay wiggled his head torch and pretended to peer into the throng of children who never stopped carting rubbish. "Oh, I'm sure she'll be there. Though I doubt you will ever recognise her under the dirt. And you'll have no time to go looking. As soon as you're on the platform, you will have to work if you want to stay alive."

"Why are you doing this?" Balvan repeated, his face crumpled with grief.

Sanjay began to herd them along the path around the pit.

"That is for Mr Ranbir to explain. You will see him before you go to the pit. Now walk on."

And they had no choice but to walk around the ledge, towards the wall with the chute.

CHAPTER EIGHTEEN

"Waiting had been a trial. But the ensuing years equally so. It was hard for me to witness first-hand the deprivation of man. We angels should work harder to guide them."

Sanjay forced them towards the chute.

As they got nearer, Tally saw a flight of steps leading up to where the mouth came out of the rock. They ascended in single file.

The stairs ended on a landing. Ahead of them, cut into the rock wall, was an arched door and between it and the wall of the chute was a golden statue, taller than two men, which Tally recognised as the Indian god Ganesh. His elephant head towered above the wall of the chute, and behind him Tally could hear the litter rustling and creaking as it oozed past, before sloshing down on to the children below.

The two henchmen opened the door and stood back for Sanjay to push Tally and Balvan into a chamber the size of a cathedral. The men slammed the door behind them and immediately the stench from the rubbish, smoke and steam cut off. Tally drew in gulping breaths and heard Balvan doing the same.

At the same moment, the sense of Jophiel's loving wings, which had surrounded her and filled her with courage, vanished, leaving Tally cold and terrified. She shrank against Balvan as she stared wide-eyed in front of her.

Columns sculpted out of the rock seemed to be holding up the ceiling of this new cave. There were two more doors, one on each side of the hall, and out of one came two men with shaven heads and orange robes. They began to scatter petals along a path lined with more life-size statues depicting Indian gods. Incense burners emitted an aroma of sandalwood that cleared Tally's airways from the stench of the pit, but also made her eyes water.

Tally's gaze followed the monk-like men. They reached a pool that took up the back portion of the cavern and threw the remaining petals onto the surface where they bobbed and danced in the ripples. The pool was fed by a waterfall flowing from the roof which formed the entire back wall of the shrine. Why didn't it overflow?

Tally raised her eyes to the waterfall - and froze. Suspended in the water was the shape of a vast dragon. It looked like it was made of glass, which shimmered and dazzled. The back of Tally's neck started to prickle, and as she stared the dragon's glowing eyes slowly blinked.

It was alive! And its gaze was boring into her soul, striking her with inexplicable grief. She couldn't look away from its malevolent stare and the images of pain and suffering reflected in its depths.

A heartrending wail from Jophiel broke the spell.

"*Jophiel!*" Tally called desperately. "*Jophiel, hear me. And stay hearing me till I tell you to stop,*" she added, hoping it would work.

But the only response was a gentle vibration from the pendant and the faintest whisper, as though he was far away. "*The power is stronger than me. I cannot help you, Tally.*" She barely made out the last words before they faded into the distance and the pendant stilled.

Did he say he couldn't help? Had he gone forever? Tally's chest tightened with terror. If her immortal angel was overwhelmed, what evil were she and Balvan about to face?

Tally clutched at Balvan's arm as they stared at each other in alarm. Balvan's face showed that he had felt the grief from the dragon's stare too.

"So, you don't cry before Vritra?" The voice came from behind. Tally spun round. As she recognised the clipped haircut and tailored clothes of her dad's friend, she was overwhelmed with relief.

"Raj!" she cried. "Oh, thank goodness, you found us. Is Daddy here?"

"No, and he doesn't know you are. As soon as I got the message that they had captured a blond child, I realised it must be you and I arranged for your father to be detained at the clinic with an extra shift. He thinks you are safe at home with Abha." Raj examined his immaculate fingernails as he spoke. "That should give us enough time."

"T... time for what? To escape?" Tally didn't understand. She ran to grab his arm. "Raj, the stolen children – they're all here. This horrible man," she pointed at the grinning Sanjay, "is the man I saw kidnap that little girl. He's behind it all. There are two houses and a magic fence and a secret tunnel and…" She faltered at the expression in Raj's black eyes. He was gazing at Tally with a little smile.

Raj clicked his fingers and Sanjay approached. "How many children do we have now?" Raj asked, not taking his eyes off Tally.

"More than a hundred," Sanjay replied.

"And is there enough litter coming down the river to keep them busy?"

"Oh yes, Mr Ranbir, sir. Plenty of litter."

Tally stared in disbelief. "Y…you're Ranbir? But…he's the reason we've been captured. Was it you all along?"

Raj/Ranbir didn't answer her. He spoke to Sanjay instead. "We need more," he demanded. "Our dear friend," he bowed towards the dragon in the water, "is growing in strength, and he needs more misery to fuel him."

Tally's mind was reeling. "Raj," she whispered. "I don't understand."

Raj sighed. "Oh Tally, I do so wish you hadn't interfered. Your father is my friend, I don't want to hurt him. But now you are here, I can't let you go."

"What are you going to do to us?" Tally gasped.

"In honour of your father, I won't send you to the scrapheap. Your little friend, however…" He made a gesture to Sanjay's men, who seized Balvan and dragged him back towards the door and the mouth of the chute.

Tally screamed and ran after Balvan, grabbing hold of his clothes with her bound hands, trying to pull him back. One man kicked out at her. His foot connected with her belly and she fell to the floor, winded.

"There, there," soothed Raj, pulling her to her feet. "You can watch as he goes down the chute. Then you'll realise how lucky you are."

Balvan yelled and kicked, but with his hands tied he couldn't get away. Against all these men, Tally couldn't do anything either, except watch in despair. Then Sanjay took hold of her again.

Tally kicked and screamed. She pulled desperately towards one of the shaven men who was lighting a guttering torch. "Help me! Please! Don't let them do this!"

Raj laughed. "They are deaf and mute, silly girl. And they serve Vritra. They don't care what happens as long as their god is honoured."

Raj and Sanjay dragged her up a slope to a gallery that looked down on the chute and its grizzly destination. Then she saw the henchmen grappling with Balvan on the landing to the stairs. They hefted him up between them and heaved him over the side just as Raj exclaimed, "There he goes!"

Tally froze in horror as Balvan slithered down the chute in the thick gunge, fighting to keep his head above the surface. His arms flailed in the air because, small mercies, they had untied his hands. Tally didn't think he would have survived otherwise.

Balvan's descent didn't take long. He was heavier than the seeping flow and he slid through quicker. As soon as he landed in the gully, a dozen hands plunged towards him and helped him clamber out. The children, their eyes huge with misery, silently patted Balvan down with grimy hands to check he wasn't hurt.

Suddenly a tiny girl dressed in rags let out a wordless wail and pointed at the river of garbage. At once the children left Balvan and converged on the gully, heaving out the rubbish that had started to build up while they were distracted.

Balvan looked up at Tally, his face a mask of terror. Then he turned away to join in the battle to keep the island clear of the filthy trash so they wouldn't be pushed over the edge.

Tally swallowed a sob of despair and called for Jophiel in her head.

Nothing.

She put her hands to her chest. The pendant was in its place. But what good was it without the angel? Never had she felt so alone.

And so betrayed.

She turned to Raj with blazing eyes and let her temper rip.

"You're a monster," she raged. "How can you do that? How can you treat children that way? And why?"

She wanted to beat him and kick him, scratch his face, and tear out his trimmed hair and beard. Oh, how she wanted to hurt him. And Sanjay. And those other two thugs.

She thought of her pin and how it had always calmed her fury. Well, she didn't need calm now – she wanted to attack these horrible men.

And she did. She flew at them with all the rage of a disturbed hornet, but they just laughed. Sanjay picked her up and flung her over his shoulder, like the sack he'd carried earlier.

Defeated and winded, Tally hung down his back, too distraught to do anything.

CHAPTER NINETEEN

"As I passed from hand to hand, compelled to follow the wearer of the pendant wherever they went, privy to their shameful secrets, their petty lives and trivial concerns, I began to appreciate the need for wisdom, understanding and judgement."

Sanjay didn't put Tally down until they were in another antechamber, off the main shrine. This room was also hewn from the rock and resembled a large living room. It felt bizarrely ordinary compared with the pit of horror or the gleaming dragon-temple; there were soft chairs, a polished refectory table and a dozen or more wooden dining chairs.

Sanjay set her down on one of these.

Raj took another, pulling it round so he sat facing her. "What shall I do with you, hmm?" he mused.

"You can let me go," Tally shouted, trying to stand up. "Along with all the children." She was fizzing with anger now. The sadness and despair had dwindled.

Raj sighed and pushed her back onto the seat. "I don't have to explain myself to a child, but if you are to stay alive, you need to understand. So I will do you the honour of revealing my work to you, young lady. After all, you either need to beat us or join us." He smiled again. "And I can assure you that you will not beat us."

"Don't bet on it!" Tally retorted.

"What I am doing will change India forever," Raj began. "I will purge it of all pollution and filth. Cleanse it and start afresh. And I know you find litter as offensive as I

187

do." He chuckled. "Your father told me it's the one thing in India you hate."

She couldn't deny that, and what he said sounded good in theory. Pollution needed tackling; but not by kidnapping children and making them slaves in an underground river.

Raj rubbed his hands together. "In a few days the streets of India's cities and towns will be clean. The countryside will be pristine, there won't be a scrap of rubbish anywhere. India will be glorious again. And I will reign over her."

Tally frowned. "How? By tipping it all into that pit and making children clear it up?" That would take forever. The rubbish would never stop, the children would die and more would be brought in… Would Raj continue till every child in India was in that cave, knee-deep in trash and starving?

Raj scoffed. "Of course not, girl. This garbage is only from Agra. It comes down the Yamuna River and plays only a tiny part of the big plan. No, I will wash away ALL the rubbish of India."

He must be insane, Tally thought.

"We are almost ready," he gloated. "The dragon you saw in the waterfall is the god Vritra. And I, Raj," he thumped his own chest, "summoned him. He is amassing the water from every river, every lake, every watercourse across India, and we will use this to wash through the cities, towns and hamlets. We will sluice away the filth and India will be free from pollution."

"But what about the people?" whispered Tally.

Raj shrugged. "Some will drown, I regret. But most will survive to live in *my* new country. I will make India resplendent again."

Tally couldn't get her head round the horror. It wouldn't just be some people who drowned, surely? Children playing on the streets, unable to run away in time; old people who couldn't run to higher ground; men working

189

in the fields who had no warning. How could that be right?

"There must be another way," she ventured. "Can't you just teach the people? They're always going on about it at home. Education, clean-up plans, getting communities to do litter pick-ups."

Raj roared with laughter. "It would take years to educate the people to change their ways. I will cleanse India in ONE DAY. Do you see the magnificence? You should applaud me – everyone will when the country is pristine. They will herald ME as the greatest hero our country has ever known – maybe the greatest in the world!"

"But if you can do that, why are you bringing garbage here? And torturing children?" Tally protested.

Raj glared at her. "It has taken me years to invoke Vritra," he snapped. "You don't just make a phone call and a god appears to do your bidding. Vritra thrives on tears, sorrow and despair. I needed the children's desolation for him to grow and become powerful enough to perform this feat. Their misery feeds Vritra. I needed a way to keep them in that state of misery, so their pathetic wails and desperate attempts to stay alive would make my beautiful god strong." Raj talked as if there was nothing cruel about it. "What more fitting than sifting through the very litter that they and their families have created?"

Tally's stomach heaved. "And will you let them all go when you've done your cleansing?" she asked.

Raj shrugged. "If they survive, I'm sure they'll be able to return to their families. And they will have learned a valuable lesson for future generations. In the meantime, I regret, I must keep them in despair." He brought his face close to Tally's. "And I still want to know how you overcame Vritra's power enough to pass through the bamboo fence."

To divert his attention, Tally made a big show of twisting her wrists and wincing at their bonds.

"Oh, my poor girl, you must be in such pain. Look how the rope has caused your delicate skin to blister." Raj waved Sanjay over. "Cut these bonds."

Tally was stunned. How could he act so kind and caring when he was torturing all those children? And he'd just sent Balvan down the chute. It was beyond belief.

"Here, let me see." Raj examined her raw skin with his doctor's expertise, after Sanjay cut the ropes and set her free. "I will bring you some ointment when I come back," he soothed, letting go of her wrist.

"You're leaving?"

"Just for now. When it is all over, I will take you back to your father. I will honour you both as guests in my new India. I must get back to the hospital. I told your father I was collecting emergency supplies and that I would check on you." Raj smirked, making Tally cringe. "Well, that part is true! I will tell him you are extremely fine, doing your lessons and missing your honoured father. But you understand he is busy, and you will wait patiently for his return."

Well, that was one small mercy; at least Dad wouldn't worry about her (though he'd be furious that she'd disobeyed him again). A glimmer of an idea lifted Tally's spirits for a second - maybe Abha would raise the alarm when Tally didn't come home for dinner?

But Raj dashed that hope with his next words. "I shall also call at the house and tell Abha that you are at Balvan's house, with your father's permission, and she can go home. She is an honourable woman. I shall save her."

"When is the flood going to be?" Tally asked.

Raj narrowed his eyes as he looked at her. "Soon," he muttered. "We're nearly ready, but I have told you enough. You will stay here in this room, on this chair."

He barked an order at Sanjay, who produced some rags out of his sack.

"Don't worry, my dear," Raj crooned. "We won't use that nasty, scratchy rope again. Keep still like a good girl."

Sanjay pinned her forearms to the arms of the seat while Raj fastened the rags around them; they did the same with her feet around the front legs of the chair. Raj stroked her hair, making her want to retch. Then he, Sanjay and the two henchmen left, leaving Tally trussed up without even her angel to comfort her.

CHAPTER TWENTY

"My task is infinite and protracted. I am condemned to help one person at a time and obliged to remain hidden. Each bearer of the pendant may know me but cannot reveal my presence or it will be my undoing. I continue to dodge demons, fiends and dark forces. Better to hide from them than engage in battles I cannot win."

Tally listened to the men's voices fade as they strode away. She hoped they *had* all gone. What if that one returned for the pendant? But no, she'd told him she'd left it back in the cave under the house.

She didn't believe Raj would take her to her father, nor that he would allow the kidnapped children to return to their parents. For a start, they all knew who he was, and their parents weren't likely to applaud him and treat him like a hero.

Another horrifying thought occurred to her; the cavern was underground. Surely all the water would flood into it and drown them?

She struggled against her bonds and instantly wished she hadn't. The strips of rag cut just as much as the rope had as she tried to manoeuvre herself into a better position.

Miserable though she was, she was better off than Balvan. And he was in this mess because of her. She had to save him instead of just sitting here. But what could she do?

"You could escape." A glorious voice rang in her head.

"Jophiel!" Tears of relief stung Tally's eyes as the angel appeared beside her, the light from his magnificent wings reflecting off the rock walls. "You came back!"

"I never went away," he responded.

"But you *did* go! You disappeared."

He lowered his head. "Yes. I'm ashamed to say, I hid. I recognised Vritra, and I quailed. We have crossed paths in the past, and Raj is deluded if he thinks he is controlling the demon. Vritra is a cruel and powerful force, pure evil. He hasn't yet reached his full strength, but when he does, he won't to bow to Raj. He will have his own plan."

"But *you* can fight him, can't you?" Tally implored. "You're an angel!"

Jophiel hesitated. "It would be the most dangerous thing I have ever undertaken, child. If I do not win, at best he will slay me, but more likely he will capture and enslave me. Either way, you and all of India will be lost."

"So, we sit here and wait for Raj to come back. And do nothing," she finished bitterly.

"Certainly not," he chided. "At least, we can get you out. Once you are free, you can run for help, warn everyone."

"Does that mean you can do something? Physically, I mean?"

"No, it doesn't," he regretted. "At least, not in the way you want. But, as usual, I can help you help yourself."

Tally frowned. "I don't think my pin will help in this situation." Did his eyes flicker at the mention of the pin? "And anyway, I can't reach it." She nodded towards her bound hands.

"You can escape from your bonds."

"How?"

"They have attached your feet to the legs of the chair, but below the cross bar. If you tilt the chair onto its back legs, you can slide your feet down and the loop will come off. Try it. But get nearer to the wall first, so you don't crash to the ground."

Tally lost no time. She bounced and shunted along the floor till she had her back to the wall with enough space to tilt the chair. She pushed.

The front legs came up into the air while the wall stopped her from falling. It was a struggle to slip her legs downwards because she wasn't tall enough. She had to push her bottom forwards on the seat to reach, which almost toppled her, but she managed it and soon her legs were free. She let the chair down with a thud and wriggled her ankles.

"Now what?" she said. "I can't run very far with a chair attached to my bottom."

"No, but now that your legs are free, can you stand and reach this jagged piece of rock here?" He pointed to the wall behind her.

"I think so!" Tally stood. The chair attached to her back was like a tortoise's shell and prevented her from straightening up completely.

But she was at the right height to saw the bonds of one arm across the razor-sharp projection of rock. Sweat ran into her eyes and she panted with the effort of moving the chair along with her arm, but she could see the rag fraying and before long she had sawn through. Her right hand was free; she quickly undid her left.

Tally flung the chair and the rags away from her. Now for the way out. She tilted her head. When had the sound of falling water got so much louder? The floor and walls were humming with vibrations, and the air was filling with a soft mist.

Tally looked at Jophiel and trembled. The light from his wings had dimmed. "What's happening?" she gasped.

Jophiel shuddered. "I am battling to keep Vritra's evil at bay, Tally. To give you time."

Tally didn't need Jophiel to explain to her that it was draining him of his energy: the way his magnificent feathers were wilting was proof enough, but she could see he wasn't going to give up.

They needed to go!

"Which way?" she demanded.

"I fear the only way out of this chamber is through the temple." Even Jophiel's voice sounded weaker than it had a minute ago.

Tally ran to the door, opening it a fraction to peek out.

The huge waterfall had doubled in volume and the noise of it was filling the cavern. With a jolt Tally realised water was spilling out of the pool and across the floor. It was already sloshing around the ankles of the monks, who were oblivious to it as they stood in a trance before the transparent dragon.

Vritra! Tally gulped. His outline reared sharply against the spume and his eyes were gleaming like twin moons, his teeth bared.

"Yikes!" Tally yelled above the crashing water. "The chamber is nearly flooded. And the dragon is twice the size!" She shot back as the water forced the door open and began to soak her shoes and the bottom of her trousers.

"Then my efforts were in vain," Jophiel cried. "Vritra's power has grown. There is no time, Tally. Vritra has tricked Raj. His strength is complete, and he is poised to attack. To save yourself, to save the children, you must defeat Vritra."

"Me?" Tally backed further into the room as the water deepened.

Jophiel's light flickered, then steadied. "You will not be alone. I will help you."

"But you said he was too dangerous." Tally had to raise her voice above the increasing din of falling water in the shrine. "And I'm just a kid! What can I do that you can't?"

"It's what we may achieve together that counts, child. Maybe, just maybe..."

"Tell me!" she shouted, drenched to her knees now.

The angel shook his head and spoke urgently inside her head. *"Surprise is our only hope. You must get as close as possible. I cannot help you get there, and I cannot stay visible. If Vritra sees me too soon, he will be able to overpower me and all will be lost. Keep the pendant under your clothes till you are right in front of him, then pull it out and summon me."*

The water was swirling hard now, and Tally was almost swept off her feet. She grasped the rough wall and stared at Jophiel in horror.

"I have faith in you, Tally. You can do this. I promise!"

Suddenly Tally's heart soared. She was invincible. She *could* do this. Though quite what 'this' was…

"What do I do when I get there?" she cried.

"You obey whatever order I give you, without hesitating."

And he disappeared into the pendant.

CHAPTER TWENTY-ONE

"My power is limited. I can influence the person who bears the pendant, and our bond is strong. But I cannot control all of mankind. That would give me power akin to the Almighty. I strive to extract the best qualities from my bearer. Their love and loyalty feed my strength."

Tally's heart banged and thumped in her chest. She fought through the swirling flood to the door.

In the shrine the water was deeper than ever, and churning round the waists of the monks who had retreated from the pool but continued to stare at Vritra.

The transparent dragon was thrashing in the cascading water. His head reached the temple ceiling and his eyes burned with fire. He was monstrous, and he roared with the noise of a hundred waterfalls.

Tally was sweating and her limbs felt like concrete. She wasn't sure she could take another step. How was she going to reach the dragon? She wasn't up to this, wasn't brave enough; she was no match for a dragon-god and a crazy man. She would have to give up…

"Yes," hissed the surrounding air. "Give up, little girl. Surrender! I am invincible. No one challenges the mighty Vritra!"

Tally covered her ears with her hands, but the voice resonated inside her head.

"Soon," it rang, "I will cleanse all of India. No humans will ever again foul my clean waters. I will rid India of every puny life form and make my rivers and lakes the jewels in my crown." His voice thundered round the shrine. "I am VRITRA! I will reclaim India for myself. No humans will roam its lands henceforth. I will recall the asuras and we will rule forevermore."

Tally crumpled against the doorframe and pressed her fists into her eyes. Suddenly cries and wails from the kidnapped children pierced the crashing of the water.

They were going to drown!

Gathering her strength, she sucked in a deep breath and launched herself into the deeper water. The flood threatened to topple her, but she propelled herself along by grabbing hold of the line of statues. When she reached the monks, she stormed between them.

Surprised, they grabbed at her, but she ripped free. The wailing increased, but she ignored it. Fighting against the strength of the flood, she charged up to the waterfall yelling, "Jophiel!" while trying to free the pendant from under her tunic.

A crack ripped through the chamber like an explosion. The air sizzled. And the dragon burst from the water and landed in front of Tally, whole and solid. His vast bulk sent the water crashing away into the gigantic chamber, where the children, in danger of being washed away, wailed harder. The dragon swelled and grew, his scales gleamed like jet, dripping and hissing with steam.

He was enormous.

He was terrifying.

And he was about to engulf her.

Tally's burst of courage deserted her. She made one last effort to pull out the pendant while uttering weakly, "Jophiel."

The dragon tossed his gigantic head from side to side and bellowed. "Yes, Jophiel! Where do you hide, Angel? Do you think I don't know you are here? Do you think *you* are going to stop me?"

Jophiel's voice roared in Tally's head. *"Take out the pin!"*

Vritra loomed over her, his eyes smouldering. He threw back his head with a grating screech. She fell to the ground. This was the end. She was going to die.

"*THE PIN,*" thundered the angel again. And with the last of her strength, Tally slipped her nail under the tip of the dressmaker's pin and drew it out of the scabbard on the angel's back.

Instantly, Jophiel appeared beside her, taller than she had ever seen him before, blazing with light. In his hand flamed a gigantic sword of fire. His wings unfolded and reached the ceiling, sending droplets of water flying.

Tally's courage rocketed at the sight and the sword flared even brighter and stronger. The angel swept it through the air towards the dragon's neck.

But Vritra swerved. He reared back, turning his glittering eyes towards Jophiel.

"Now I have you," he mocked, his words echoing off the walls. Jophiel's light dimmed, his wings folded, and he seemed to shrink. Suddenly the pin was back in Tally's hand, tiny and cold and useless. Tally screamed.

Vritra was going to defeat her angel. She had to do something. She lunged towards the dragon's belly – the only part she could reach – and thrust her puny little pin into his scales.

The air exploded with the dragon's laughter as he bent his head to devour her in one gulp. But in doing so he exposed his neck.

Jophiel blazed like a volcano, the sword flashed once more in his hand, brighter than flame, and with one almighty swoosh, he decapitated the river demon.

CHAPTER TWENTY-TWO

"My adventures and experiences are too many to record here —
they span thousands of years.

I have adorned the necks and have influenced the lives of the
great and the good, the meek and the humble. The only way in
which their troubles differ is in proportion."

Tally squeezed her eyes shut as she waited for the vast
head to fall on her and shower her in blood.

Nothing. There was silence; and when she dared peek,
there was emptiness. The dragon had disappeared. The

monks ran towards her with their hands stretched out. Tally braced herself to be captured again, but they raced past without even a glance and fled out of the door they had come in through.

Tally turned to Jophiel. His shoulders were slumped, his wings folded loosely against his back. He seemed smaller and dimmer, and Tally wanted to run and hug him but didn't dare.

Instead, she whispered, "Are you all right?"

The angel raised his head slowly, his expression full of wonder. "Am I all right? Do you know what you did, my child? You saved an entire continent. Never mind a very humble angel."

"Well, I… um…" she faltered. "Do you mean Vritra's dead? Just like that? But *you* defeated him, not me."

"I merely wielded the sword you created," he said. "Evil is a strange power. Pure love can often defeat it. Your action was selfless. You acted for me, driven by love. You were so brave!"

Tally didn't feel very brave. And all she'd done was stick a silly pin in – well, in a dragon's tummy. She felt a giggle start in the bottom of her own tummy. It was so STUPID! The giggles multiplied. Jophiel smiled with her. That made her laugh more, and then more, till she was giggling so uncontrollably she could barely breathe.

Till a bucket of icy water tipped over her head.

"Not again!" she protested, raising her hand to brush her wet hair out of her eyes.

It *was* wet.

"Not me," exclaimed Jophiel. And they looked up to see water cascading through a crack in the ceiling. "We need to leave this shrine," he cried. "The caves are still flooding. Come on!"

As Tally burst onto the landing where the men had hefted Balvan into the chute, she saw that the water and rubbish was cascading down in a torrent. The children on the island below didn't know that their greatest enemy had been defeated. While bailing frantically, they were screaming and clinging to each other's hands as they fought against being swept off the island into the pit of flames.

A group of older boys and girls were trying to take charge. They had armfuls of rags and they were pointing up to the chute. One of the filthy, bedraggled figures looked familiar. It was Balvan.

"Balvan!" Tally screamed. "We killed Vritra!"

She may as well have screamed under water for all the effect it had. Despairing, she looked at Jophiel.

"Shout again," he ordered.

As Tally opened her mouth, Jophiel filled the cavern with a flash of white light that shocked everyone into silence. The children stopped moving and looked up, some of them shielding their eyes. Tally used the silence to shout. "Balvan! Over here."

Balvan ploughed through the litter and crowds to the edge of the island nearest to her. "Tally!" he yelled. "You're alive!"

"Yes," she shouted back. "And Vritra is dead!"

As Jophiel reduced his light to a gentle glow, Tally continued to shout. "We have to get you out. The caves are going to flood."

But Sanjay had said there was no way off the island.

And the river was running faster now, fed by the waters that Vritra had summoned from all corners of India. Then she saw Balvan gesticulating. He cupped his mouth and shouted, "We have rope ladders! The kids have been making them from the garbage for months. We just need you to catch the end of a rope and pull them up."

Tally gulped. Gymnastics had been her thing, not ball games. She wasn't sure she would catch a rope flung across a void. And even if she caught it and secured it, how would the littler ones climb across? It would be so dangerous. They could fall into the flames at the bottom of the pit.

Balvan was waving at her again. "Come to the bottom of the stairs," he yelled. "The gap is narrowest there."

As Tally started down the stairs her brain raced. If she
could get onto the bottom of the chute and fix the ropes
there, the children wouldn't have to cross over the fire pit.
But how to get onto the chute? She couldn't reach it from
the walkway.

She frowned. What if she started at the top? From the
landing where the men had thrown Balvan over? Then she
could climb down to a point low enough to catch the
ladders.

Tally felt the pendant tremble at her chest.

"Trust me, Jophiel," she whispered, and she signalled to
Balvan to wait. Then, deafened by the crash of falling
water and debris, she turned and sped back to the landing.
The water had risen in the shrine and was starting to
cascade down the stairs. She fought her way against it to
the statue of Ganesh, terrified of being washed off the
stairway.

As the water rose almost to her waist Tally was able to
grab the lowest of one of Ganesh's four arms, and then use

the other three and his trunk to clamber up onto the rocky sides of the huge slide. The river of waste was still rushing down the channel. She tried not to look. And she wished she didn't have to breathe – it was so gross.

Tally braced herself to descend. It's just like being on the bars at the gym, she told herself. Don't look down. And, turning to face the rock, she lowered herself from one foothold to another, like scrambling down the banister of a staircase.

The harsh rock ripped the flimsy silk of her trousers and grazed her skin, but she didn't think about the pain. The noise of the water worried her far more, and she clung to the rocks with hands made slippery through sweat and fear. She was desperate not to be swept away in the torrent of rubbish and filthy water. Thankfully, Jophiel's light continued to glow beside her. *"You're doing so well, child,"* he murmured inside her head. *"You're almost there."*

Tally risked a glance down into the sea of kids who had fallen silent and were staring upwards. She was still about twenty feet above them, but she could see Balvan. She met his gaze, and he nodded. She'd gone far enough.

Tally turned around, carefully. It was precarious, but she straddled a lump of rock and sat facing the pit with her hands free to catch the rope. She prayed it would reach.

A tall, skinny boy had taken Balvan's place at the front of the crowd. He held the end of a line made of rags in his right hand. More boys and girls, standing next to him, cradled piles of similar looking material which she supposed must be the ladders. The first boy swung his rope backwards and forwards over his head, while screwing up his eyes to calculate his throw. Tally focused on the knot at the end. That was what she had to catch.

"Help me, Jophiel," she prayed.

"You're fine," he encouraged. *"Pretend you are playing ball, sitting in the garden. It doesn't matter if you miss a few times. You only need to catch it once."*

Tally tried not to think about all the children relying on her; the rubbish which was building up so fast; the raging swell of the river above.

As the rope came flying towards her, she flung out her hands, but it wasn't close enough. She didn't dare lean out that far. The boy tried again. And again, and again. On the fifth try, she caught it! She held tight to the knot and scouted around for the most prominent rock. Wrapping the end of the rope around it she stared, aghast.

"I don't know how to tie a knot," she wailed. "At least, not a proper one. I only know a reef knot."

"*I once had a friend who was a fisherman, child,*" Jophiel soothed. "*I will guide you.*" And he appeared briefly beside her, floating his hands above hers, showing her where to make the loops, cross the ends and tie them so they were secure.

"*You don't need me now, Tally,*" he whispered, "*You know what to do.*" Then he slipped back into the pendant, out of sight.

Tally flipped the ladder, so it lay on the chute rather than on the jagged stone wall. Then she signalled to Balvan that all was ready. The noise of the water was getting stronger, and her heart thumped. Would they get out in time? There were a lot of children.

They *had* to get out in time.

A girl's head appeared at the end of the chute first. She battled with the stream of water and rubbish, then managed to get one hand on the rock and haul herself clear of the water onto the wall. Tally raised her hand in triumph and the girl nodded. She held another rope ladder, and she tied that on too. Then, hand over hand, she climbed up the edge of the chute towards Tally. Behind her another head appeared, and a boy heaved himself up, securing another rope. Soon children were appearing in a constant stream.

Tally turned and clambered faster and faster back to the landing and the statue. She showed the girl how to climb down Ganesh's limbs.

"That's it, you're safe now," Tally encouraged. "Head through that door to the one on the other side of the shrine." The girl looked at Tally, not understanding, so Tally pointed. She nodded, but as Tally darted back up to help some younger children over the wall, the girl stayed to lift them off before leading them away.

Soon children were coming so quickly that Tally was getting in the way, so she slid down to stand in the icy, swirling water and direct them to the door in the shrine.

Suddenly one of the children grabbed her arm. It was Balvan! He swung her round and engulfed her in a stinky hug.

Then she felt a tugging on her tunic and looked down to see Aditi, eyes shining out of a face plastered in muck.

Ignoring the stench, Tally flung her arms around the little girl, lifted her off her feet and twirled her around. All about them, children were reaching the top of the chute and jumping off. Balvan grabbed her and Aditi's hands and they ran to make space for the constant stream of refugees.

"How do we get out?" he panted.

"I'm not exactly sure," Tally admitted. "We can't go the way we came. I've been sending everyone to that door over there. It's higher than the rest of the cave, so I just hope it will lead up and out."

At that moment, a distant rumble made everyone freeze. The pendant trembled against Tally's skin. The rumble turned to a roar of water hurling itself along the underground river, crammed with rubbish and mud.

"Quick! Get everyone out now. There's no time to lose," Tally yelled, as the flow of water pouring out of the shrine doubled.

They turned and battled through the flooded temple. The churning water dragged at their clothes, making it impossible to run. Children shouted and screamed as they fought desperately to reach the door. Balvan hoisted Aditi onto his back. At the same moment, a small boy was knocked off his feet beside Tally, and she just managed to grab his hand before he was swept away. All around them, older children carried little ones while everyone shouted in alarm.

"Keep moving! Don't stop!"

CHAPTER TWENTY-THREE

"I do my best. My reason for being remains to represent judgement, wisdom and understanding. This is my cause, and one I have learned to embrace, though I still hide from the Creator lest he should cast me to live with Lucifer. I tremble that he should discover me unless he is ready to forgive me."

Tally and Balvan pushed the last of the children ahead of them through the door that led into a tunnel.

Tally hesitated. What if this wasn't the way? What if they were just running to another trap – more floods, more rubbish, or those men?

Behind her, the chute began to overflow. The rubbish cascaded over the sides and joined the water in the temple. Statues toppled and churned in the currents. Balvan and Tally's eyes locked in horror. There was no choice; they ducked into the tunnel behind the rest of the children.

The noise of water and screaming children was deafening. And it was pitch dark. Tally fought through the water, terrified she would never see daylight again.

Gradually, though, she realised the going was getting easier. The water was receding, the floor was rising. The tunnel led upwards!

And the light was increasing. It wasn't as dark as the passageway Sanjay had brought them down: a bare electric bulb hung from the ceiling above and shone a weak light.

From then on, every twenty metres was another bulb. The level of water sank to ankle height and continued sinking. The noise of children screaming in terror changed to one of children chattering in relief.

As they forged ahead, Balvan asked Tally what had
happened in the shrine after they had thrown him down
the chute. Between breaths, she told him about Raj's Big
Plan to rid India of litter; how, by summoning Vritra and
his powers, he had been planning to set himself up as ruler
of the country; how even he had yet to learn that Vritra
was mightier and had intended to wipe out everyone.

"But what happened to Vritra? Did you defeat him?"

What should she say? She couldn't tell him about
Jophiel, but if she told him she'd stuck a pin in a dragon,
he'd die laughing. Anyway, it wasn't her pin that defeated
Vritra, it only distracted him. It was Jophiel's celestial
sword that ended the evil.

Balvan looked at her sideways. He brought his lips to
her ear. "Is it something to do with your special power?"
he whispered.

Oh yikes! She'd forgotten about that. Before she could
answer, he became very solemn and asked, "Are you an
angel, Tally?"

"No!" she protested. "Of course I'm not an angel. Do I look like an angel?"

"Well, for a moment, when you were fixing the ropes on the chute, you looked like you had wings," he insisted. "We all saw you."

Obviously, Tally realised, they must have seen Jophiel when he had appeared to guide her. "There was so much happening," she countered. "Water running, fires burning. You don't know what you saw."

Balvan looked sceptical. Tally had to convince him they were mistaken.

"If I was an angel, do you think I would have wasted time climbing down that chute? I'd have just flown down and grabbed the rope." She needed to change the subject. "Where did the ropes come from, anyway?"

"We are Indian," he declared. "We can make anything. The older kids had been saving any fabric that got washed down and weaving it into ropes to make ladders. They had hoped to form a human tower to attach it to the chute.

But the flow of the water and the rubbish was always too fast. They weren't able to cease clearing long enough to practise."

Suddenly the optimistic chatter of the crowd became calls of alarm from ahead and the line stopped moving.

"What are they saying?" Tally asked, grabbing Balvan's arm.

"They can't go any further. It's a dead end."

Dead end. Tally's heart dropped. She had been dreading a locked door, even barred. But a dead end? Now what?

They couldn't go back. The temple would be completely flooded by now, and if the water kept coming, this tunnel would flood too.

But the children surged backwards in panic and Tally and Balvan had to retreat to avoid getting crushed. Their feet splashed into water again and Tally's heart pounded.

Suddenly Balvan grabbed her arm. "Look up there!" he cried, pointing to the ceiling. "In the rock. I think it's a trapdoor!"

Tally squinted through the low light to where he was pointing. It did look like a trapdoor.

"Can you reach it?" she gasped.

"Not on my own! Here, get on my shoulders and I'll hoist you up." Balvan crouched down for Tally to climb onto his shoulders, steadied by the children standing around them.

Tally pushed with all her might against the trapdoor. At first it wouldn't budge, but she wouldn't give up. She heaved and heaved till her shoulders burned.

Finally, the square wooden slab lifted. Tally heard a screech of metal as whatever was above slid off, followed by an almighty crash. Instantly a shaft of bright artificial light streamed through the gap into the tunnel.

Tally shoved the slab further away and willing hands pushed her through the opening. To her utter astonishment, Tally's fingers touched smooth linoleum. The electric light bouncing off the walls dazzled her, but she continued to haul herself out.

She looked around, confused. She seemed to be in a large, almost empty room. No sign of Raj or his men, thank goodness. Just a metal filing cabinet lying on its side. Opposite her was an open door and through it she could see a wide corridor. Tally stared in amazement. There was a sign on the wall: *X-ray this way*.

She was in the hospital!

Tally shouted down to Balvan and immediately half a dozen taller boys and girls clambered through, and, with Tally, started pulling others up. Soon they were streaming out like lava from a volcano.

The children blinked in the unaccustomed glare and stared round the room in confusion.

"Go!" Tally yelled, pointing to the door. "Just run and get help." She knew it would cause an enormous shock to anyone they encountered, but at least they would be safe.

At last, Balvan, who had been pushing from below, clambered up with Aditi. The three of them joined the throng of screaming kids surging through the basement corridors to reach the main part of the hospital.

Tally and Balvan, with Aditi clinging to her brother's T-shirt, pushed their way to the front just in time to see several medics rushing towards them.

One or two bemused visitors turned at the noise, then recoiled from the stench rising from the garbage-soaked rags of the kidnapped children.

The orderlies shouted questions. Tally didn't need to know Hindi to understand they were asking for explanations which Balvan was hurriedly providing.

As the children clamoured around, adding their stories to Balvan's, Tally spotted a flash of movement ahead. A well-dressed doctor came out of a nearby ward to see what all the commotion was about… and walked purposefully away from the chaos.

Tally grabbed Balvan's arm. "Quick," she urged, "there's Raj!"

They broke free from the crowd and took up pursuit. Raj slowed to allow some nurses with a patient in a wheelchair to pass and Tally shouted, "Ranbir!"

Raj paused and looked back. It was all Tally and Balvan needed to catch up. Balvan launched himself in a flying tackle just as an orderly came round the corner with a laundry trolley. Raj landed on the trolley and Balvan landed on top of him.

The orderly yelled at Balvan and tried to pull him off.

"Call the police!" Tally shouted. "This is the man who's been stealing all the children."

"Don't be ridiculous," snapped Raj, struggling to get out from under Balvan. He was about to succeed, with help from the confused orderly, when four more of the kidnapped boys and girls came round the corner and flung themselves onto the pile, taking the orderly with them.

Other staff came running. Tally pleaded with them to call the police.

"Stop this at once," commanded one doctor, in English.

Tally turned to her, rushing to explain. "Please! I promise you, he's the kidnapper. He called himself Ranbir and held all the children captive in caves under here. Look," she pointed to Raj's trouser cuffs, "he has dust on his trousers the same colour as on mine. It's from the tunnels Please believe me!"

Before the doctor could answer, dozens more kidnapped boys and girls rounded the corner, shouting and pointing at Raj. The staff had to fight to stop them all flinging themselves onto the now cowering doctor.

"Just check in the basement storeroom," Tally implored. "You'll see the trapdoor that leads to the caves. That's where we've escaped from."

The doctor nodded to an orderly who ran to check. In the meantime, Balvan extricated himself from the pile of angry children holding Raj down. He grinned at Tally, then he caught her arm and pointed. "There's your dad," he cried. "Let's go to him."

"No!" Tally gasped and yanked Balvan through the nearest door. Fortunately, it was a broom cupboard, not a ward full of very sick people. Aditi slipped through with them.

Balvan looked confused. "Why don't you want to go to your father?"

"He must never know I was involved," Tally told him. "If he finds out, he'll send me straight back to England – to boarding school."

Balvan laughed. "Tally, no. That's crazy! You are a hero. You will be famous all over India – all over the world when the news gets out. He'll be so proud of you, he'll let you do anything you want."

"No," Tally insisted. She wouldn't expose Jophiel, and she refused to take credit for things she would never had done without him. "You don't know my dad. He must never find out. It's not that I'm frightened of him, it's just that I know he'll want to keep me safe." She fixed Balvan with a wild, beseeching stare. "Help me get back to our house and promise me you'll say nothing? Swear it, I beg you."

Balvan pursed his lips but nodded. Aditi took her hand. "I don't want you to leave," she whispered.

Tally knelt next to her. "So you must never say anything, Aditi," she said fiercely. "Do you understand? Tell them Raj kidnapped you, tell them all the things that happened to you, but never say I was there."

Aditi nodded, her eyes solemn. Her brother blew out his breath. "I can't believe you want to keep this secret," he grumbled. "Everyone will want to thank you. My parents will want to give you the world. You'd be so famous!"

"Well, there is one thing your mum could do for me." Tally pointed at her ripped clothes. "Do you think she would sew an identical replacement for me? I don't know how I'd get the money for it, but I'll never be able to explain to Dad how my clothes got in this state."

"You don't need money." Balvan was curt. "My mother will make you a cupboard full of new clothes for nothing."

He took hold of her hands and stared into her eyes. Tally's tummy and heart did a funny little jump, as if they were trying to swap places. "You are the bravest person I have ever met."

Tally blushed. "We'd better go," she muttered. "I need to get back."

They opened the cupboard door and peeped out to make sure it was clear.

Tally could see a cluster of older children talking and gesticulating to a group of security guards. Nurses were helping the weaker children onto trolleys. Police had already arrived and were holding a shame-faced Raj between them, while dozens of children clamoured to tell of the events underground.

The temple and the cavern would be flooded now, Tally thought. Would Raj/Ranbir's crimes stay hidden forever, or would the word of a hundred or more children convince the authorities they were real? As long as no one else summons Vritra...

Tally could see her dad on the edge of the group. He had his back to her.

"This way," she whispered to Balvan and Aditi.

The activity around the rescued children made it easy to slip out unnoticed. They exited the hospital and started the long trek back to Tally's house.

CHAPTER TWENTY-FOUR

"The man who gifted me to Tally's mother carried me for forty years. He was an explorer and took me back to Sinai, to see for himself the cave where my image was created. As soon as we saw Tally's mother gazing at the walls of St Catherine's Monastery, he understood we had to say goodbye.

He handed me to her without a word."

As soon as Tally got home, having said goodbye to Balvan and Aditi and promising to see them tomorrow, she tore off her filthy clothes and had a shower. She was exhausted and famished, but she needed to be clean first. She washed her hair four times to get rid of the stench from the pit. Then she pulled on a long-sleeved T-shirt and jeans to hide the rope-burn marks on her wrists and ankles from her dad.

She wanted to go to bed, but it was still only early evening, and she knew if Dad came home and found her asleep, he'd want an explanation. So she just lay on top of her bedspread.

Most of all, she wanted to call Jophiel. Something about the way he had retreated into the pendant frightened her. She wanted to talk to him. She closed her eyes and held the figurine as if it was glass. It was cold and hard.

"Jophiel," she whispered.

Nothing happened. There was no infusion of warm light, no feeling of love and joy. Just darkness.

"Jophiel," she tried again, louder. Still nothing. She swallowed a tear. Had he gone? Forever? "Please, Jophiel," she sobbed. But there was no answer.

Tally curled into a ball and tried to calm her pounding heart. Did angels die? He had told her it would destroy him to reveal himself. And yet he had done just that in the pit, to help her with the knots. Had it destroyed him?

Or was he so tired he couldn't hear her?

Or had she imagined it all? Maybe he didn't exist, had never existed. Maybe she'd conjured him up like a small child does an imaginary friend.

She threw herself onto her other side. She couldn't imagine life without him. And if she'd created him with her imagination, why didn't she just bring him back?

No. He *existed*. Mum had said Tally would know when the time came for him to leave, and she would give him freely. Well, she didn't feel like that. She wasn't ready to let him go.

Sleep overtook her, and she woke with a start when the front door slammed. She jumped up and put her hand to her chest. The pendant was still cold.

Tally heard Dad rushing to her bedroom and as soon as he saw her, he slumped against the door frame. His haggard face scared her.

"Dad! What's happened? Are you OK?"

With two steps, he crossed the room and almost suffocated her in a bear hug. "I was so worried about you," he mumbled into her hair.

"Why?" Tally's shoulders slumped. He must have heard she was one of the children who appeared in the hospital.

Dad collapsed onto the bed beside her. "Three of the strangest things have happened," he started. "First, the kidnapped children have all reappeared, not two hours ago, in the hospital. It was so bizarre – one minute there was the usual hospital buzz, the next a hundred filthy kids are tearing through the corridors, screaming and shouting. Someone said there was an English girl with them, and I was so worried. But here you are, safe. I can't tell you how relieved I am."

She wasn't out of danger yet. "Yep, here I am," she said quickly. Then, to steer Dad away from risky ground, she asked innocently, "But why were the children filthy?"

"Well, they said they'd been held in caves under the hospital and forced to clear mountains of litter. But the second thing, the most unbelievable thing, is that the person behind it all was Raj." He shook his head as if still trying to get his brain round the thought. Tally let out her breath. He'd bought it. He would have questioned her much more closely if he really thought she'd been there underground, rescuing all those children.

"He was my friend," Dad said in a voice full of disbelief. "When they led him away, he babbled something about cleaning India and ruling the world. And to think I trusted him to come and check on you. Anything could have happened!" He peered at her. "He didn't try to make you leave the house, did he?"

Tally shook her head and urged him on. "Tell me what happened! How did they find the children? Are they all

OK? What about Aditi?" she remembered to ask at the last
moment.

"I don't know. I wanted to get straight back to you.
We'll call in the morning and see if she has returned." Dad
stood up. "I'm not sure how the children escaped.
Apparently they were being held prisoner on an island in
a pit. Right under our noses! Can you believe that?" He
shook his head again. "They're all insisting there was a
devil in there with them and that an angel saved them. No
one can get any sense out of them."

Tally stared at her feet to hide her smile.

"Anyway," Dad rallied. "The wonderful thing is *you* are
OK." He ruffled her hair, and she pulled a face.

"I thought you said there were three things," Tally
asked.

"Oh yes! You know that lake with the hotel on it?" Tally
nodded. "Well, all the water has vanished. Just poured
into the ground."

"Into the caves?"

"I presume so. Lucky the children got out in time. Anyway, how have you got on with your schoolwork?" came the next question, and Tally knew she was safe.

"Um, I haven't quite done all the set work," she muttered. "I've been looking up things about ancient Indian Gods and how to tie a good knot."

Dad laughed. "You are a funny thing. All that adventure, and you missed everything. I hope you're not too disappointed. Let's have some supper and you can tell me about your day."

He held out his hand, and they went into the kitchen to forage for food. He queried Abha's absence, so Tally invented a family emergency that had called her away.

Dad ran his hand over his eyes. "Do you mean to say you were all alone when Raj came round to check on you?" She winced but said nothing. "I'm not happy about all this, Tally," he continued. "We should leave India."

"Dad, no!" She almost dropped her fork in her anguish. "We've only just arrived," she argued. "We haven't even been here two weeks yet, and we've hardly seen anything because you've been so busy at the hospital. Please let's stay. Please?"

"I'll think about it overnight," he promised. "But don't get your hopes up."

Tally wasn't giving up that easily. "I just feel that there's so much to learn here. We've barely scratched the surface. Balvan and I were talking this morning about getting a group of kids together from his school and starting a litter cleaning campaign…"

Dad raised his eyebrows.

"Yes," Tally rushed on. "They don't have community projects here like they do at home. We want to start one of our own."

"Wow." Dad whistled. "You really have thought this through, haven't you?"

"Well," Tally said. "There have been a few things that made up my mind, actually. There's just so much litter here, isn't there, Dad? And I bet lots of people would help clear it up."

Dad was staring at her, his face softening. Tally pushed her last point.

"And Mum would have wanted me to do whatever I could to give something back. Wouldn't she?" she ended in a small voice.

Dad buried his face in his hands, then looked up. "You are so much like your mum," he whispered. "Yes, she would have wanted to do exactly the same."

Tally held her breath.

"All right then, we'll stay!"

Tally leapt up and threw her arms around him.

"I love you so much, Daddy," she mumbled into his chest. And they stayed like that, hugging, till she dragged herself away to bed.

CHAPTER TWENTY-FIVE

"And should it come to pass that the Creator forgives me, would he reinstate me?"

Tally got ready for bed before she attempted to call Jophiel again. She lifted the pendant and stared at the timeless face of her angel.

"Are you there, Jophiel?" she whispered. Nothing happened. The pendant remained lifeless.

She lay on the pillow, staring at the ceiling through tears that burned. Then they dazzled. She sat up and wiped her eyes with her hand. The dazzling light was still there, and it was coming from the sky, outside.

Was it fireworks? A fire?

Before Tally could get out of bed to investigate, the light was filling her room. It was bright, warm, full of joy.

And then Jophiel stood before her. Tally had to shield her eyes: his robes glowed as white as a frozen lightning bolt. His wings brushed the ceiling and sent a shower of sparks as they moved. Tally had never seen him look so resplendent. She turned her face away from his blazing light. Awed and humble, she wanted to hug him. But how do you hug a light? Simultaneously, she wanted to fall to her knees before him.

He was MAGNIFICENT.

"My child," he said.

She found her voice. "You're back."

"For now."

Her eyes filled with tears again. "Have you come to say goodbye?" She had thought she would have years before she had to let him go. It was like losing her mum all over again.

But she would be brave. Jophiel knew what he had to do. She trusted his judgement.

She fiddled with the pendant. "Do you need this?" she asked in a tiny voice.

Even though Tally couldn't make out his face, she knew he was smiling. "Are you so eager to part from me?"

Hope filled her. "You mean you're not leaving after all? You'll stay?"

"I will. I have chosen to stay."

"Can you explain?" she ventured.

"No."

Tally picked at the bedclothes to fill the silence. "Dad said we'll stay in India for a while."

"I know." His light shimmered like a shiver. "I am thankful for that. I did not want to board another aeroplane quite so soon after the last time."

Tally giggled, then sobered. "He said I remind him of Mum. Do you think so too?"

"Oh yes," he agreed. "She would have been so proud of you today."

"You did most of it," Tally insisted. "And anyway, I had no choice. It was act or die."

"Oh, you had a choice," Jophiel countered. "Just as I had a choice whether to appear before hundreds of children who will grow to tell the tale or remain hidden in safety. But your love and your loyalty strengthened me. And you proved them even further after your heroics in the caves."

Tally was confused. "After? What did I do? I just came home."

"Exactly. You kept my secret, and you considered your father's feelings rather than seek fame and fortune."

"It was so he wouldn't pack me off to boarding school," she admitted.

"No," Jophiel said. "It wasn't. Had he learned of your heroism, your father would have granted any wish. You knew that. Your motives were pure, Tally, regardless of what you told Balvan. I know your heart. And your loyalty to me was equally fierce, for to tell your story, you would have had to tell mine. You *chose* to remain silent."

Tally looked toward his shining face. He nodded at her and his entire being glowed his approval.

"I love you," she whispered.

"I know."

She lay down with a contented sigh. She closed her eyes, and a gentle hand stroked her hair, just as Mum used to do.

"Will you stay forever?" Tally whispered.

"No, child. But the day I leave you, you will feel only joy at letting me go. You will meet someone who needs me, and you will understand. In the meantime, I have no doubt there are many more adventures to come!"

"Really?" said Tally. "Can you see into the future?"

Jophiel's laugh was the sound of cathedral bells. "No, Tally. But I can see into your soul, and I know you will seek adventure wherever we go.

And I will be beside you."

The End

Have you enjoyed
Tally and the Angel?

If so, please write a review!
**Authors love to hear from their readers.
It takes a long time to write a book and there's
nothing better than hearing from readers who have
liked it.
Not only that, it helps other readers, children, parents
and grandparents find the story.**

**You can let Eleanor Dixon know how much you
enjoyed Tally and the Angel by leaving a short review
on Amazon, Goodreads or your preferred online
store.**

If you're under age 13, ask a grown up to help you.

**AND DON'T FORGET – be sure not to give away any of
the story's secrets!**

COMING SOON...

Tally and Jophiel's adventures don't finish here.
Look out for
Book Two: Canada

.

You can check for updates on Eleanor's website:
eleanordixon.com
On Instagram: theburreauinthefield
Or on Facebook:
Eleanor Dixon@theburreau

ACKNOWLEDGEMENTS:

My thanks always go first to Shaun, my husband, who is incredibly supportive.

Then to Vicky, my editor who is incredibly encouraging.

Rob has been incredibly patient while we try to find the right cover.

And Digit, Mokey and Moji (my two dogs and cat) are just plain incredible!

What would you expect around the story of an angel as incredible as Jophiel?

Printed in Great Britain
by Amazon